Hooky Hefferman is ordered by his dominating aunt in Hove to visit the Cotswold village of Barwold. The young daughter of an old friend of hers is thought to be keeping bad company there.

Meanwhile in the nearby Cotswold town of Dunsly one of the local newsagents is going dangerously mad. Inside his head he receives instructions from 'The Lord' who ordains that he shall cleanse the neighbourhood of the local whores. He strangles Dolly Winter – that is the first murder. Dolly is buried in Barwold where she was born. The goings-on in Barwold obsess more than one character in the story, and in the midst of this suspicion and the crimes that follow is Hooky himself.

Hooky appears to be devoting his time to the saloon bar in the local pub, where certain very interesting characters spend much of their time. But he is not a private investigator for nothing, and he takes note of some curiosities of behaviour and some discrepancies. He also finds himself at odds with the local police.

Hooky is in fine exuberant form in Laurence Meynell's new novel, which gallops cheerfully along while its sinister plot unfolds towards a satisfactory climax.

by the same author

THE CURIOUS CRIME OF MISS JULIA BLOSSOM
DEATH BY ARRANGEMENT
A LITTLE MATTER OF ARSON
THE FATAL FLAW
THE THIRTEEN TRUMPETERS
THE FAIRLY INNOCENT LITTLE MAN
DON'T STOP FOR HOOKY HEFFERMAN
HOOKY AND THE CROCK OF GOLD
THE LOST HALF HOUR
HOOKY GETS THE WOODEN SPOON
PAPERSNAKE
HOOKY AND THE VILLAINOUS CHAUFFEUR
HOOKY AND THE PRANCING HORSE
HOOKY GOES TO BLAZES
THE SECRET OF THE PIT
SILVER GUILT
THE OPEN DOOR
etc.

THE AFFAIR AT BARWOLD

Laurence Meynell

MACMILLAN

ISBN: 0 333 37974 8

First published 1985 by
MACMILLAN LONDON LIMITED
London and Basingstoke
Associated companies in Auckland, Dallas, Delhi,
Dublin, Hong Kong, Johannesburg, Lagos, Manzini,
Melbourne, Nairobi, New York, Singapore, Tokyo,
Washington and Zaria

Typeset in Great Britain by
BOOKWORM TYPESETTING LIMITED
Manchester

Printed and bound in Great Britain by
ANCHOR BRENDON LIMITED
Tiptree, Essex

CHAPTER ONE

On that particular Tuesday I felt an urge to escape from the town and to get out into the Cotswold countryside. This meant leaving my wife in charge of the shop, and although Eileen isn't very bright she is perfectly capable of looking after the business for half a day and she knows how I like things run.

It isn't a big business. I don't want a big business. And anyway Dunsly wouldn't support a big business; Dunsly-by-Dutton to give the place its full name, a small stone-built Cotswold town which after being sleepy enough through the winter comes to life when tourists start arriving in the spring.

The newspaper part of the business keeps pretty constant throughout the year, and in the spring and summer there's quite a good trade in what I call the knick-knack side – picture postcards, stationery, pens, pencils, sweets, china mementoes and the like. A useful bit of money also comes in from the notices in the glass-fronted case outside the shop. I charge forty pence a week for these and Eileen says if I wasn't particular about the sort of notice I allow there the glass case could do a great deal better. I daresay it could; but I *am* particular; the Lord tells me to be particular; there are certain magazines I won't stock and certain advertisements I won't display, and that's an end of it.

On this particular Tuesday I wanted to walk over the fields to Barwold, although I didn't tell Eileen that I was going there of course.

Barwold is a village tucked away in the valley of the Bar, that's the river which, small though it is, dominates all our countryside.

I call Barwold a village, it would be better to say 'hamlet'. I like the word hamlet. I like the small, simple things, not the mess which money and motorcars have made of the world.

'You've no ambition,' Eileen says; well, she doesn't actually say it because she is afraid of me; she knows that the Lord works through me and this makes her afraid of me; but she thinks it. She's a woman and that's the way women *do* think. That's the way their minds work. More, more, more. More of everything. More money, more clothes, more sex.

Of course she is quite wrong. I have plenty of ambition; ambition to do what the Lord lays on me to do, but naturally I keep my thoughts about that to myself.

It was a lovely spring day and, luckily, to get to Barwold from Dunsly it is hardly necessary to keep to the road at all.

The first half mile is up the long steady slope of Dunsly Hill, which must have been hard collar-work for horses in the coaching days. That is road work, of course, and you can't escape it; but at the crest of the hill there's an old-fashioned iron stile on the left-hand side and once you are over that you have said good-bye and good riddance to the road.

Now you can stop wondering whether you are going to be run down by an overtaking motorcar and start thinking your own thoughts.

I had plenty to think about. Eileen's stupid brother for one thing. I don't say that Eileen's brother was the principal thing in my head that spring morning; he wasn't, I had something else far more important to think about, but he occupied my thoughts for a time because Eileen was so upset about him. When she gets upset the atmosphere in the household suffers and I don't like that. I don't like an

6

unhappy atmosphere in the house so I thought for a bit about Eileen's brother and wished he hadn't got himself into such a silly mess. Over some woman, of course. You can be quite sure of that. A woman wanting something from him – clothes, money, sex.

'If he gets into real trouble,' Eileen nerved herself to ask, 'and wants any help I suppose we couldn't—?'

'No, we couldn't,' I told her flat. I work hard for what little money comes my way and I don't intend to start handing it out to lame dogs like Eileen's brother. If some woman had got him into money difficulties let him deal with her as she ought to be dealt with. So 'No, we couldn't,' I told Eileen and whether she liked it or not she had to accept it.

So that disposed of Eileen's brother and his troubles and I was free to think about other matters; about how lovely the day was for one thing. Cotswold snow loath to go, the saying is round here; but when it does go, when at last the spring does come to these parts it comes in a glorious burst. I do believe the wind blows fresher on these Cotswold slopes than anywhere else, the sun shines more sweetly. For a few moments you believe in Paradise, but then you start thinking about men and women, about what a mess they've made of things and about the shameful things they get up to; the things the Lord wants them punished for, and you forget about Paradise.

The path I was following ran along the top edge of a huge sloping field, and if I looked to my left below me I could see, scattered about, a flock of the famous Barwold Baldfaces. Everybody knows why the Lord Chancellor of England has to sit on a woolsack and it was wool from the Barwold Baldfaces that originally filled that sack. It was the proceeds from selling that wool which built most of the Cotswold churches.

Already I could see a glimpse of the square tower of Barwold church, grey amid the green of the churchyard yews; there was some activity going forward in the churchyard but I was too far away to be sure of the details of it.

Presently the path I was following ceased to be a mere footpath and, after I had pushed my way through a broken-down gate, became a borstal which in turn, a quarter of a mile further on, blossomed out into a sunken lane, the high banks on each side already splendid with primroses. Inevitably, men, and particularly women, being the stupid things they are, this was known to Barwold people as Lovers' Lane and it brought me in time to the first house in the village.

This first house, a good solid stone-built early Victorian affair known as Otter Lodge, had recently changed hands and now there was a sign outside it which read:

Barwold Antiques, High-class Furniture,
Pictures, Silver. Inspection invited.

Private houses turned into antique shops are no new thing in the Cotswolds. Perhaps it is because of a feeling at the back of everybody's mind that the end is getting close and that there isn't much future to look forward to; perhaps it's just the result of watching too many programmes on the thing I won't allow Eileen to have in the house, TV; whatever the reason, people nowadays are obsessed by the belief that anything old must be valuable. And the word 'old' is conveniently stretched by the dealers who have somehow managed to make the nineteen-twenties sound like pre-history.

My own shop back in Dunsly depended a good deal on the tourist trade and if the same tourists were silly enough to be had for mugs over so-called antiques I suppose it wasn't up to me to grumble.

Some of the pieces for sale in Otter Lodge were standing outside in the small front garden and I stopped for a moment to take a look at them. The price tags made me laugh and confirmed me in my view of what fools most people are. I was on the point of moving on when the door of the house opened and a woman came out into the warm spring sunshine.

She was wearing so little that for a moment I thought she was naked. She saw me looking at her over the low front hedge and she laughed. She couldn't have cared less. Brazen, that's what all these women are nowadays, going about near enough naked, showing their bosoms and bottoms off to everybody. Brazen. They flaunt their nakedness.

When she caught sight of me standing there staring at her this young woman wasn't in the least disconcerted and when she spoke it was in one of those high-pitched aristocratic voices, the I-belong-to-a-different-world sort of voice which I always find particularly irritating.

'If you want to look at any of the furniture,' she said, 'the house is open, but please don't just stand there doing a Peeping Tom act at me.'

This made me angry. Sometimes I can get very angry indeed, it comes over my mind like a red cloud; people think that because you are small (I'm only five feet four in height) you can't get angry. That's a very silly mistake to make. The arrogant way this woman spoke to me made me angry now. To be accused of being a Peeping Tom when I was thinking that she ought to be horsewhipped for flaunting her nakedness! But I kept my temper, just. 'I'm no Peeping Tom,' I told her in a steady voice.

'Then sod off,' she said, and laughed.

The house door opened again and two men came out each carrying a glass. Husband and lover most likely I supposed.

The woman turned to say something to them – some remark about me I shouldn't wonder – and they all burst out laughing.

Nobody bothered about me any more. I didn't belong in their fornicating, drinking world; I didn't exist. I turned away from Otter Lodge and went on my way towards the church.

9

I'm not a churchgoer. The antics parsons get up to seem just plain silly to me, theatrical. I don't have to go into a church to find out what the Lord wants me to do. When the Lord has work for me he tells me privately and I do it; but all the same there is nothing more satisfactory, more lovely, than an English church standing in its green and quiet churchyard in the middle of an English village. When I got near to the lych gate I could see that the activity I had spotted from far off had developed and a funeral was going forward. It seemed to have attracted rather more attention than one might expect in so small a place as Barwold, but then, one way or another, everyone is interested in death.

The coffin was resting by the open grave; the parson's white surplice was fluttering in the spring breeze; a little group, perhaps a dozen, of the intimate mourners made a black smudge against the green of the churchyard grass; further off, at what I suppose they would call a respectful distance, the inevitable group of lookers-on, the gawpers, was gathered. I could have passed by and taken no notice; but I didn't; I joined the gawpers.

The parson was enjoying himself. Well, why not? I thought, it's a good, fat theatrical part and he's doing justice to it. 'Man that is born of woman hath but a short time to live,' he droned, 'and is full of misery.'

You can say that again, I thought, what with rent and rates and the gas bills all going up and it taking three weeks even to get to see a doctor on the National Health; but in spite of all that I didn't feel miserable; the spring sunshine was too warm to feel miserable, the wind blew too sweetly. I was alive and well and above ground, so I wasn't feeling miserable.

'For as much as it hath pleased Almighty God of his great mercy to take into himself the soul of our dear departed sister,' the parson went on and then came the dust to dust, ashes to ashes bit; I glanced round the gawpers to see how they were reacting. Pretty stolidly on the whole. I supposed that most of them were fellow villagers who had

10

come 'to show respect'. All they were really feeling was relief that it wasn't their turn yet.

After any funeral, the feast. It's a natural reaction so I wasn't surprised to find the bar of the one Barwold inn, the Ram, doing good business.

I'm not a heavy drinker, far from it; but I enjoy my modest half pint; and especially I enjoy drinking it slowly and quietly in the corner of a crowded bar watching all the other people there swilling away and laughing and talking loudly and generally making fools of themselves. I just stand in my quiet corner watching them, wondering about them, making up tales about them, imagining things.

Presently the door opened and two of the people from Otter Lodge came noisily in, the girl who had told me to sod off, now wearing a little, but not all that much, more, and one of her companions. A tough-looking character this, but with the sort of face you felt you could trust somehow; 'Too good for that bitch,' I thought. Presumably the drinking session at home was finished and these two had come along to the local to start another one.

When the two of them got up to the bar I was near enough to hear the tough-looking character give his order. 'Two Pimms Number One,' he said. Armed with their tall glasses they moved away to a table by the window and in doing so caught sight of me.

The woman turned and said something in that high-pitched voice of hers which made the man laugh. I guessed what she was saying. She was saying, 'That's the little so-and-so I told to sod off.' All right my naked beauty, I thought, laugh away, maybe one of these days you'll be high and mighty once too often. . . .

I finished my half pint and since it was a hot day, and something of a special occasion, I asked the young chap behind the bar to give me the other half.

'You're busy,' I said.

'There's been a funeral this morning,' he explained, 'and that always helps.'

11

'A funeral? Anybody special?'

'A girl called Dolly Winter. No better than she should have been by all accounts and got herself murdered by some man in Dunsly; but she came from these parts originally and so of course people are interested.'

I nodded. Dolly Winter. I was certainly interested. I killed her.

CHAPTER TWO

Some time before Dolly Winter, the murdered prostitute, was buried in Barwold churchyard a man with an unmistakably military stamp about his upright carriage and a precise way of walking was making his fastidious way through the jungle of Soho.

Lieutenant Colonel Henry Fellingham didn't care much for Soho. He was well aware, human nature being what it is, that human beings get up to all sorts of curious antics. If that's the way we are made so be it, he thought, but for heaven's sake why flaunt it all in public? To flaunt anything in public was bad form in Harry Fellingham's book and he disliked bad form intensely.

He was looking for Gerrard Mews following the some-what hazy directions about how to find it given him by an autocratic old lady in Hove. Harry Fellingham didn't in the least resent the Honourable Theresa Page-Foley being autocratic. In his opinion the old lady had every right to be autocratic, she had autocratic connections and was of the old school. She was of his world, and although that world might for all practical purposes have vanished it was much more agreeable to pretend that it hadn't.

Eventually between the dustbins and the sleazy sex-shops Fellingham came to the entrance of the cul-de-sac known as Gerrard Mews; at the far end of that unattractive backwater stood the building which in its day had been a pleasant enough family residence – Regency House.

If Regency House had possessed a hall Roly Watkins would, perhaps, have been dignified by the title of Hall

Porter. There being no hall he was content to be watchdog, messenger, emergency plumber, part-time carpenter, provider of dubious racing tips and generally indispensable guardian angel of the place.

In response to the Lieutenant Colonel's query Roly said that he thought Mr Hefferman was in and would go to make sure.

He could have communicated with Hooky Hefferman's abode on the first floor by means of an old-fashioned and highly insanitary speaking tube, but Roly reckoned himself a great judge of character and he had instantly formed the opinion that the Lieutenant Colonel was an unusual visitor to Regency House and one about whom Hooky should be forewarned.

'Stand to attention,' he said as soon as he got inside the room. 'Smarten yourself up, guv.'

'What the devil are you talking about?' Hooky demanded.

'A military gent wants to see you. A toff. Lieutenant Colonel Fellingham. Seems harmless but you never know with these army types. I remember—'

Hooky had not the slightest desire to hear what his henchman remembered. Roly's reminiscences were picturesque, usually patently untrue and apt to be unending, and Hooky knew most of them by heart.

'Never mind what you think you remember,' he advised briskly. 'Tell the Lieutenant Colonel that in spite of being extremely busy I can spare a few minutes to learn what he wants, so will he please come up.'

Roly grinned broadly; to his certain knowledge no business had come the way of Regency House for the past three days.

'I'll let the Colonel know how busy you are,' he said, 'and if I was you I'd put the *Sporting Life* away, it'll look better.'

Invited to sit in a somewhat ramshackle chair, offered a drink which he declined, and a cigarette which he accepted,

14

Harry Fellingham studied the man opposite him with interest.

He was inclined to like what he saw.

A six footer. Broad shoulders. Features which missed being good-looking but which were humorously alert, the sort of face you felt inclined to trust; altogether, Harry Fellingham judged, the sort of fellow who would make a good friend and a bad enemy.

'I understand,' Harry Fellingham said, 'that you are what I believe is called a Private Investigator, is that true?'

'The truth generally needs a bit of elaboration to get it right,' Hooky answered cautiously. 'P.I., yes, and that really means that I'm a sort of Citizens' Advice Panel, a Bureau for Missing Persons and a Father Confessor rolled into one.'

Harry Fellingham smiled slightly and said, 'You don't look much like a father confessor to me; but I am told on very good authority that you are the right person to deal with my particular problem.'

'I wonder who told you that?'

'A Mrs Page-Foley. Theresa Page-Foley, who is, I understand, your aunt.'

The mention of his aunt's name immediately alerted Hooky to the importance of the visit. It would not be too much to say that it alarmed him. The Honourable Theresa Page-Foley was an alarming person. When fiats were issued from the flat in Hove in that spiky Edwardian handwriting they commanded attention.

'You know my aunt?' Hooky prompted cautiously.

'I have known Theresa Page-Foley for, let me see, twenty-two years. A remarkable woman. Of course she is older than I am, almost a generation older, but I have always had an immense regard, indeed it would not be too much to say an immense affection, for her.'

Hooky eyed his visitor with increased respect; brave chaps these military types, he thought.

15

'It was twenty-two years ago that I first met your aunt,' Harry Fellingham went on, 'at one of old Lady Allmaster's receptions. That was the year my daughter, Tessa, was born and your aunt agreed to become godmother to the child. On her own terms, of course; she was as outspoken about the matter as you would expect her to be.

"If you want the child brought up in the Christian faith," she said, "you will have to see to it yourself. I'm not much of a Christian. I once spent three months in Rome and that cured me of that. What are you calling the child? Tessa? I like the name. I'll give Tessa a good piece of silver and as far as I am concerned that will be all."

'Since it was your aunt who was doing the giving the piece of silver was indeed a good one – a splendid George the Third coffee pot from Regent Street. My wife polishes it every day. That was twenty-two years ago, Tessa's no longer a child; she is a young woman and a problem. It was about Tessa that I went to see your aunt.'

In his day Hooky had known a number of young women of twenty-two who could be described as problems; he wondered what Tessa's own particular method of kicking over the traces might be.

'You'll be thinking,' Harry Fellingham went on, 'that I'm cut to a stereotyped military pattern; that, seen from the standpoint of twenty-two, I'm an old fogey anyway and that it's natural enough for young birds to start flapping their wings. You'll be thinking along these lines, I imagine.'

Hooky grinned; he found himself liking this decent little soldier.

'Something like that,' he confessed.

'Quite right. Up to a point. But there are complications. Tessa's mother for one thing. Nancy's ill. She herself doesn't know just how ill she is, but I know because the doctor has told me. But even if she doesn't know, she suspects, she wants all the love and affection round her that she can have.

'She's not getting much love and affection from her

16

daughter; nor is she likely to. It's a dreadful thing to say, and I don't pretend to know why it should have come about, but the fact is that the girl actively dislikes her mother; I believe she actually hates her.'

Fellingham looked at Hooky with sad eyes and spread his hands in a little gesture of helplessness.

Hooky felt sorry for him; but he felt even sorrier for himself. Reviving the dying, or dead, flames of filial affection was not a mission he fancied.

He was cheered up by Fellingham's next words.

'One thing you clearly can't do, one thing nobody can do, is to make Tessa act like a dutiful and loving daughter. The wind bloweth where it listeth, isn't that what the good book says? You can't command love so I'm not asking you to go off on that wild goose chase, but even if I can't get love for Nancy I desperately want to stop her from being hurt, and I'm afraid that the sort of life Tessa is living now is likely to end up in hurt for everybody including herself.'

'Hitting the high-spots is she?' Hooky asked and immediately felt slightly ashamed of the flippancy.

'I don't know exactly what she is up to,' Fellingham answered, 'and that's what I want to find out. What I do know is that she has taken up with a man called Lynton Hadleigh. I suppose they are living together. I'm old-fashioned enough not to like that, but it seems to be the normal thing these days and I suppose one has to accept it.

'By chance the other day at the Club this man Hadleigh's name cropped up in conversation and I learnt a good deal about him. Well bred and well brought up, apparently – if you call going to Harrow being well brought up which personally I don't; and now, according to this fellow at the Club, no better than a waster. At any rate there are ugly rumours about the man; he seems to have inherited some money and to be doing dubious things with it.

'Apparently his latest venture is into the world of antiques; the man who told me this said that in his opinion half the people dealing in antiques are dishonest and quite

17

a number of them are mixed up in actual crime of one sort or another.

'I suppose Tessa is fascinated by this man; I daresay she'll get over it in time, but I am desperately anxious to find out exactly what is happening to the girl and to get into some sort of communication with her before she comes to real harm.

'It's not the slightest use my going after her myself, that would only make things worse. So what am I to do? That was the question I asked the girl's godmother, your aunt, a woman who has seen a lot of life and who knows a lot, a wise woman.'

'If you want somebody who is used to mixing with shady characters and dubious company you can't do better than get in touch with my nephew,' Theresa told me. 'Tell him I sent you to him and that I expect him to do his best for you.'

Confronted by this message from the High Priestess at Hove, Hooky felt that he had little option, but even without strong words from his aunt he would have been inclined to accept Harry Fellingham's commission; Hooky liked the little man and felt sorry for him, blessed as he was with a wife dying of cancer and a daughter who apparently couldn't care less.

He asked for details and was given virtually none. 'I can't tell you details,' Fellingham said, 'it's details that I want to find out. All I know is that the two of them are living in a place called Barwold, somewhere in the Cotswolds I believe, and that they have set up in the antiques business there.'

The next morning Roly Watkins watched with amused tolerance whilst his employer climbed aboard Matilda – Matilda beloved by her owner as being one of the oldest and best preserved Jags still on the road; mocked at by the factotum of Regency House – not a car-minded person – as being a 'mechanical bag of bones'.

''Ow far did you say you were going?' he demanded.

'Somewhere in the Cotswolds.'

To Roly Watkins, a metropolitan animal if ever there was one, the name 'Cotswolds' conjured up for him visions of huge spaces and unimaginable distances.

'Well, good luck to you,' he said, 'but I doubt if you'll make it. If you're not back in two or three days I'll send out a search party. What are you after? Big game is it?'

'I'm going to the assistance of a lady,' Hooky said.

Roly shook his head. 'We'll need the search party then,' he said. 'You never learn, do you guv?'

Navigating by guess and by God, and preferring, as he always did, unfrequented by-roads to juggernaut filled motorways, Hooky arrived eventually at Barwold.

Matilda made light of the Cotswold hills; she hurried when she was asked to; she purred along easily when Hooky wanted it that way, she behaved like the perfect lady she was.

When Hooky finally came to a halt in Barwold's little square he gave the car an affectionate slap. 'Well done old girl,' he said, and the thought crossed his mind that if all the ladies of his acquaintance had been as dependable certain episodes in his life would have been a good deal easier; but on the other hand, he was bound to admit, considerably less picturesque.

Police Constable White watched the stranger's arrival with an indulgent smile. 'Bit on the antique side isn't it?' he asked.

Criticism of his beloved Jag always riled Hooky so he reported sharply with 'Perhaps you've forgotten about Cleopatra.'

'Cleopatra? PC White's unpoetical mind was at a loss.

'Age did not wither her, you may recall,' Hooky pointed out, 'nor custom stale her infinite variety. Is there a hotel in this place?'

'There's the Ram, on the other side of the square. It's not exactly a hotel, more of a country inn, but they do put people up occasionally.'

19

'Well, as you apparently have nothing to do,' Hooky said amiably, 'you might see that young vandals don't start messing about with my antique car whilst I'm in the pub getting fixed up.'

'We don't have much in the way of young vandals in Barwold,' PC White assured him, 'and there's always plenty for the law to do.'

George Dawson and Mrs Dawson, his mother, kept the Ram. George, a good-hearted fellow but with not much more initiative than a Cotswold sheep, was inclined to be dubious about Hooky's request.

Put the gentleman up? Well, he didn't really know if they could manage or if the gentleman would find it suitable – at which juncture Mrs Dawson, his mother, a dark gypsy-like woman and twice the man her son was came upon the scene, gave Hooky one long appraising and approving feminine look, and took command. Of course they could put the gentleman up and make him comfortable too, and if that was his car standing in the square with nosey Chalky White staring at it, why not bring it into the inn yard where it can be tucked away safely, and as it was past midday what would the gentleman fancy for lunch, there was a sweet piece of gammon or a Cotswold pie if he preferred it; 'But of course you'll be wanting a drink first, won't you, sir?' she enquired.

Hooky already realised that here was an excellent Christian woman with all her priorities right.

'A Pimms Number One, madam,' he replied, and Martha Dawson smiled, hugely pleased; it was a long time since anyone had called her 'madam'.

Considerably later, two Pimms and half a Cotswold pie to the good, Hooky set out to explore Barwold. Matilda was safely installed in the Ram yard and Martha Dawson had earned further good marks by exclaiming, 'That's a gentleman's car, that is; that's the right sort of car for you to have, sir.'

With this comforting asssurance ringing in his ears Hooky started off on foot.

His guess that in a place as small as Barwold there wouldn't be more than one antique shop was soon proved right, and within a few minutes of leaving the Ram he found himself at the far end of the village studying the sign 'Barwold Antiques, High Class Furniture, Pictures, Silver. Inspection invited.'

A few pieces of furniture – a table and three chairs – were on view in the small garden in front of the house, and studying the prices marked on them Hooky realised that as a hard-working, and only intermittently employed, private eye he was in the wrong business.

Inside Otter Lodge it was agreeably cool, and in spite of various transformations it had undergone the house managed to maintain a good deal of the dignity and charm it had once possessed as a Victorian home.

Hooky's entrance caused a warning bell to jangle and after half a minute interval the warning bell caused the proprietor to appear. Lynton Hadleigh in person, Hooky supposed, and he studied the man with interest.

Like the good pro that he was Hooky had his spiel ready. About antique furniture he knew next to nothing, a fact which his formidable aunt always found annoying, 'You were brought up amongst good things,' she would exclaim crossly, 'why on earth didn't some appreciation of them rub off onto you – too busy chasing the under housemaid, I suppose.'

Pursuit of the under housemaid, and later of other ladies, had not however prevented Hooky from acquiring in time a genuine liking for Victorian paintings. He had scraped together sufficient knowledge on this subject to be able to talk about it without disgracing himself; and in Otter Lodge he actually found himself at an advantage, as the proprietor didn't seem to know, or care, much about Victorian paintings. 'I'm not sure what we've got in that

21

line,' he confessed in amiable response to Hooky's query, 'Take a look round and see if there's anything that interests you.'

What Hooky found interesting was Lynton Hadleigh himself. Hooky was a great believer in first impressions and after only five minutes in Hadleigh's company he was aready beginning to realise that the impression Henry Fellingham had given him of the man would have to be drastically revised.

The Lieutenant Colonel, a disappointed father and a desperately worried husband, had been, Hooky now felt sure, way off target. Hadleigh was poor material, he realised, but not vicious material. He was the sort of weak character more likely to be a crook's accomplice than the crook himself. Macbeth with – possibly – Lady Macbeth in the background.

'Are you just passing through Barwold?' Hadleigh enquired.

'Actually I'm staying in the place for a day or two. At the Ram with the excellent Mrs Dawson, having a general look round.'

Hadleigh seemed genuinely pleased. 'You must look in again,' he said, 'whenever you feel inclined – ah, here's Tessa, she'll be able to tell you more about Victorian paintings than I can.'

When Tessa Fellingham came in a great deal was instantly made clear to Hooky. This one could tell him about a lot of things besides Victorian paintings, he thought. A good-looker. A hard, intelligent, selfish little face. A snapper-up of opportunities and a manipulator of weaker vessels if ever there was one, without an ounce of truth in her. Lady Macbeth in person. If there were any knives involved she would want to be handling them. How the devil did decent little Harry Fellingham come to breed this shrew, Hooky wondered.

'I'm delighted to meet you,' he said, and monstrous lie though this was in one way, yet it wasn't altogether a lie.

'What a charming collection of things you have here. Hefferman's my name. Hooky for short, as you will probably have guessed already.' He tapped a nose, still considerably misshapen after various misadventures.

'Mr Hefferman is staying at the Ram for a few days; he's interested in Victorian paintings and I have told him to come in at any time and have a look at anything he likes,' Hadleigh explained.

Lady Macbeth smiled. She flattered herself that she was good at summing men up.

'I'll show Mr Hefferman anything he wants to see,' she promised, and the jangling of the street door bell admitting a customer sounded like the end of a round to Hooky.

His visit to Otter Lodge had given Hooky a good deal to think about and he thought about it all that evening in a long, unhurried session at the bar of the Ram.

Trade was quiet and Mrs Dawson had plenty of time for conversation. Questioned about the Otter Lodge set-up she had not much of practical use to offer.

'London people,' she said, investing the words with a nice mixture of scorn and envious respect, 'and my word don't they just stick on London prices! What people can be talked into paying for bits and pieces of furniture that used to be kept in the attics once is nobody's business. Still, I mustn't grumble; they're good customers in here I must admit. There's nothing against a woman having a drink, I take a glass myself now and again; but that one from Otter Lodge certainly likes her gin and tonics. He pays, of course, I suppose he's got the money; but if you ask me she wears the trousers.'

Philosophy from beyond the bar Hooky thought; he had often listened to it, often disagreed with it, but with the gem offered by the good Mrs Dawson he now found himself agreeing entirely. If anybody in the Otter Lodge scenario was in need of a rescue act Hooky felt pretty certain already that it was Adam and not Eve. Eve could look after herself, and if I don't watch my step she'll be looking after me,

Hooky warned himself, having already noted and assessed an unmistakable glint in Tessa's eye. Which naturally put an edge on things and made his assignment all the more exciting.

His thoughts prompted him to say aloud, 'He who goes into the jungle will one day meet a tiger.'

Martha Dawson was puzzled. 'You say some funny things, Mr Hefferman,' she said. 'Have you by any chance any connection with the funeral?'

'*Timor mortis conturbat me,*' Hooky said. He disliked talk about funerals. 'There's one funeral I shan't be able to avoid,' he was in the habit of saying, 'and I shall go to that unwillingly; all the rest I avoid like the plague.'

'What funeral?' he enquired, not really wanting to know.

'Tomorrow morning, here,' Mrs Dawson told him, speaking with that ghoulish relish which women, so much nearer to the real heart of life, always show about these things. 'That girl Dolly Winter. I expect you saw it in the papers. Used to live here and then went off to the town and, oh dear, well these days, if you leave the door open to all and sundry you never know what's going to happen to you, do you? Well, it happened to her. And I don't suppose they'll ever find the man. How can they, like I just said, when the door's wide open and it's help yourself. Men do help themselves, don't they?'

They do indeed, Hooky thought, they do indeed, and for once in a way he felt a little ashamed of his masculinity.

The next morning shortly after eleven o'clock he set out for the jungle, Otter Lodge.

It was already a warm day and the tigress was dressed, or undressed, as though she were expecting it to be very warm indeed.

'I thought you'd be coming back,' she greeted Hooky, 'what shall we talk about? Victorian paintings? Or something else? Well, paintings to start with anyway. I've been looking some out for you.'

It suited Hooky admirably to have a pile of canvases,

some framed, some not, to sort through, and he settled in a corner of the shop taking as long as possible over what he was doing and meanwhile keeping his eyes and ears open. Every now and again the door bell noisily announced a possible customer. Once or twice a purchase was made, on one occasion to an American, for a large amount; but as often as not it was a question of looking round, mumbling an excuse and going out again.

Hooky was amused by the different reception accorded to various customers. If they looked well-heeled and had the smell of money about them Tessa put on her well-bred charming act; for ordinary tourists who had come in more or less by mistake, nosing about for cheap souvenirs, she left out the charm and sent them packing.

Hooky was just beginning to think that he could hardly extend his search among the minor – some of them very minor – Victorian artists much longer when Lynton Hadleigh came in from the living quarters of the house. He seemed genuinely pleased to find Hooky there and catching sight of the clock made what Hooky considered to be an extremely sensible remark. 'What about the mid-morning noggin?'

A handsome corner cupboard, with a warning SOLD notice on it, contained all that was necessary; and in no time at all the mid-morning noggins were produced – three large gin and tonics in three extremely elegant glasses.

Whilst Hadleigh was assembling the drinks the tigress, looking through the window, said, 'What do you suppose that little runt out there wants?'

The stranger staring at the piece of furniture in the front garden was indeed little: quite possibly he warranted the derogatory 'runt', yet Hooky studied him with interest; experience had taught him not to write off any man because of lack of inches, and the short figure out there in the sunshine looking fixedly first at the things in the garden and then at the house, had somehow something about him. . . .

The tigress opened the door and Hooky noted with

25

amusement the little man's facial reaction to her lack of clothing.

Words passed between them of which Hooky caught only her final contemptuous dismissive ones, 'Sod off then,' followed by a laugh.

The stranger hesitated for a second or so then turned and walked away. Hooky watched him and wondered about him. Some day she'll tell somebody to sod off once too often, he thought.

CHAPTER THREE

The Dunsly *Courier* ran the Dolly Winter murder story for all it was worth. For rather more than it was worth in Vic Marsh's opinion. Detective Inspector Marsh was getting near the end of his service, and what with a general shortage of men and the brashness of many of the only half-trained young constables he had plenty on his plate without the complication of a strangled prostitute.

'What about the press?' his sergeant asked. 'They've been buzzing round like flies.'

Marsh made a face. 'The *media*, as everybody calls them nowadays,' he answered sourly, 'though why everything has to change its name I don't know. Who was it who said all change is for the worse?'

Sergeant Wilson was not a Johnsonian scholar so he could only grin and shake his head. 'I don't know who said it,' he admitted 'but he wasn't far off the mark.'

'The official line is that we are actively pursuing enquiries, which incidentally happens to be true, something you can't say about a lot of the guff we hand out.'

Marsh was a married man with a normal sort of home; his wife was a bustling practical body, his two children, both towards the end of their teens, were already beginning to pose problems. As a rule Elsie Marsh studiously avoided talking about her husband's work, but on the subject of Dolly Winter she did have something to say. Like most women who have led entirely virtuous lives through lack of opportunity rather than by deliberate choice she had very little sympathy for her fallen sisters.

Marsh listened to her acid remarks without commenting on them. As far as he was concerned prostitution, and all that went with 'the game', was an established and accepted fact of normal life.

'I don't mind what they get up to in their spare time,' he had once declared, 'as long as the silly bints don't go and get themselves murdered.'

Now one had got herself murdered and Marsh had to do something about it.

There was not much difficulty in establishing some immediate facts. The murdered girl was called Dorothy (Dolly) Winter; about eighteen months ago she had moved into two rooms on the ground floor of 8 Wardle Gardens, not far from Dunsly station.

Wardle Gardens had, at one time, been in house agents' jargon a 'desirable neighbourhood'; it still retained, at least outwardly, a sort of stuffy respectability. The three-storied houses were now without exception split up into so-called 'flats'.

In number eight the top two rooms were occupied, and had been for a long time, by an old woman called Davidson who very seldom went out and who had no desire at all to be mixed up in anything involving the police. The two rooms on the middle floor were let to a couple of students who were at the local university all day and at one of the local discos most of the evening.

The ground floor flat was occupied by Dolly Winter.

On Tuesday morning, before setting out for the university, Molly James had a discussion with Arthur, the brother who shared the first floor flat with her.

She was expecting a parcel, a somewhat expensive dress, which she had orderd from an advertisement in the *Sunday Telegraph* magazine. She was afraid that this would be delivered in her absence; so would it be OK, she debated with Arthur, to ask the woman on the ground floor to take it in and look after it for the day.

They had never got further than 'Good morning, nice

day isn't it?' terms with the ground floor flat, but they decided that it really wasn't a great deal to ask and were suitably grateful when Dolly Winter agreed quite amiably to take the parcel in if it was delivered and look after it until they were back from the university.

On Tuesday evening when they got back to the flat, as it happened a shade later than usual, they found the parcel lying on the doorstep. Relief at seeing it was mixed in Molly with mild annoyance. 'She *said* she was going to be in all afternoon,' she complained. 'Be reasonable,' her brother said, 'I suppose she had to go out for something.'

The parcel was opened, the contents much admired and the incident forgotten for twenty-four hours until on returning home the following day – Wednesday – they noticed that the milk for the ground floor flat had not been taken in.

Arthur James, who had an inquisitive turn of mind, said, 'She didn't say anything about going away; I wonder if she's OK.'

The following evening – it was now Thursday – a second bottle of milk was on the doorstep and Molly said, 'I suppose she *is* all right; but had you better have a look?'

With a bit of a scramble Arthur managed to get a view through the front window. What he saw brought him back white-faced to Molly and after a few minutes' discussion they both went down to the police station in Tallon Street.

Arthur James's report of what he had seen set the routine wheels in motion and before long Detective Inspector Vic Marsh knew that he had a murder case on his hands, and this, as he was only too well aware, meant endless hopeful questions and equally endless and usually unhelpful answers; but the Q & A routine was the only one the Inspector knew and the one that had to be followed.

'How long have you known the murdered woman?' he asked Arthur and Molly James.

'Since she moved into the ground floor flat, and that's just a year ago.'

'Would you say you were friendly with her?'

'We hardly knew her. We were away at the university all day and nearly always went down to Terry's Disco in the evenings, but we certainly weren't unfriendly; no quarrel or anything like that.'

'Did you know what her profession was?'

In reply to this Arthur James said that they realised that the ground floor flat had a certain number of men callers and they had joked about it once or twice but it wasn't their business and they didn't bother about it.

Had they ever heard any sounds of quarrelling or any sort of disturbance from the ground floor flat?

'No, never.'

'You'll be carrying on at the university, will you?'

'For another two years, we hope.'

When Arthur James and his sister had left Marsh raised an enquiring eyebrow to his sergeant.

Sergeant Wilson shook his head. 'Nothing there,' was his opinion.

The inspector nodded agreement. 'All the same, a bit of corroboration won't come amiss,' he said. 'Get up to the university tomorrow and do a bit of checking. What about the old lady in the top flat?'

Again Wilson shook his head. 'She's damn near bedridden,' he said, 'and doesn't take an interest in anything. He says she's never seen any men going into the house and as a matter of fact even if she had I don't believe she'd tell us anything about them. She's one of the don't-want-to-get-involved lot.'

'The ever helpful public,' Marsh said. 'Please protect us from the dreadful crime wave but don't expect us to risk raising a finger to help you – oh well, nothing new about that, of course, it's what we are used to. Right; what have we got? A prostitute working at home – how many clients would she have in a week, Wilson?'

Sergeant Wilson looked slightly shocked. 'How should I know, sir?'

'I thought an active young fellow like you might know about that sort of thing – well, anyway, let's say a fair number of men and any one of them might have done it; by the way, anything from forensic?'

'Nothing yet; but they always take their time; they may come up with something.'

May is right, Marsh thought sadly; the popular belief that fingerprints, betraying wisps of clothing, cigarette ends of specialised brands and similar convenient clues were scattered about like confetti might be good materials for a TV series but seldom proved true in everyday life.

'Let's hope they do,' he said. 'Meanwhile how does a girl who earns her living on her back get hold of these men, these clients of hers?'

Sergeant Wilson knew the answer to that. 'Through these ads outside the paper shops.'

'Exactly. It's the ads outside the paper shops that we've got to concentrate on first, Wilson.'

Sergeant Wilson set out on his task armed with the telephone number of the ground floor flat in Wardle Gardens and with a photograph (somewhat out of date) of the murdered woman.

There were five paper shops in Dunsly and in addition four shops which did a mixed trade in postcards, Cotswold souvenirs, sweets and cigarettes.

Outside the first paper shop which Wilson tackled there was a large glass-fronted case displaying the usual assortment of cards – *Accommodation urgently required for respectable single man. Home repairs? Garden work? Anything undertaken. Reasonable rates. For sale, cheap, Colston Dishwasher. Good Condition.*

Wilson had not the slightest interest in the urgently required accommodation, in the house repairs or the Colston dishwasher but there were three advertisements in the case which took his immediate attention:–

'Young Lady seeks part-time employment.'
'ex Air Hostess seeks ground position.'

'Attractive young lady (blonde)
gives private French lessons.'

Each of these little bits of bait was followed by a telephone number. The first one (Young Lady seeks part-time employment) appeared over Tel. 32041, which Wilson knew to be Dolly Winter's number. Might be getting somewhere, you never knew your luck, was his optimistic thought as he took his burly frame into the small shop.

Optimism, he soon discovered, was hardly justified. Excited at the prospect of being concerned, however remotely, in a murder case the shop-keeper was willing, almost over willing, to co-operate but had very little of any substance to say. The cost of having a card displayed in the frame was forty pence a week, he said; occasionally a card would be put in for one week only, but people usually kept them in for at least a month, sometimes more; advertisers came in and paid over the counter in cash and it would only be by chance if he (the proprietor) knew one of them personally.

Sergeant Wilson produced his photograph.

'Did you know her?' he asked.

The shop-keeper considered the faded photograph long and earnestly. 'I don't know her,' he said at last, 'not to say *know*, but I've seen her. I saw her when she came in about the card. I remember her.'

'What makes you remember her?'

'Because she wanted her card in for twenty-six weeks and paid ten-forty for it. All the girls with that sort of card are the same. A week's no good to them, after all they're in permanent business, aren't they?'

'Did you ever see a man with her?'

'No. She just came in and paid her money and that was it.'

'Did you ever notice any men; any one man in particular perhaps, studying these prostitutes' cards?'

'I expect lots of people read them. I've never bothered to

32

notice. As a matter of fact from inside the shop, behind the counter, it's almost impossible to see who's looking at the case outside.'

Inspector Marsh heard Sergeant Wilson's account of this interview and considered it in silence for a few seconds, then he asked, 'What about the others?'

'Two of them were a bit different,' the sergeant said, 'but the rest much the same – the same girls advertising with the same cards and mostly paying in the same way. They come in once every six months, pay their money and out again. Two of the shops recognised the photograph, the others weren't sure and nobody remembers having seen a man with her!'

'You said two shops were a bit different?'

'Well, Jelf's in the Arcade for one—'

Marsh gave a wry, derisive laugh. Martin Jelf was a loudly self-proclaimed Communist who was convinced that the revolution was just round the corner and who worked unceasingly to further it.

'I don't suppose you got a lot of co-operation there,' Marsh said.

'Jelf said that even if he had known anything he wouldn't have told me and that if the police would stop their brutal harassment of the underprivileged poor they would be able to devote their time to catching the real criminals and would I please leave his shop at once as my being there was giving the place a bad name.'

The inspector nodded. 'Jelf's usual stuff,' he said; 'but I think we'll keep an eye on Red Jelf all the same. He's a fanatic and I don't know quite why but I've got a feeling that the way Dolly Winter was murdered has a touch of fanaticism about it somehow. What was the other different one?'

'Hudson's.'

For a moment Marsh looked blank.

'In North Street. Only a small place. Papers mostly and a few odds and ends.'

'What makes him different?'

Sergeant Wilson laughed and said, 'He's dead against it.'

'Against what?'

'Girls going on the game. The whole male and female business. He's got some cards outside his shop, but there aren't any of the *attractive young blonde seeks work at home* sort among them. He says he wouldn't put one up if he was paid twenty pounds a week for it. Won't touch any of it; none of the usual mags on sale either; *Men Only*, *Playboy*, *He & She* – none of that lot.'

'You seem to be well up in the titles, Sergeant,' Marsh said dryly. 'Not much good showing him the woman's photograph then.'

'None at all. I did show it to him, but he wasn't interested. Didn't know anything about her, and didn't want to.'

We were both in the shop when the detective called. Eileen was re-arranging the souvenir shelf – not that it needed any re-arranging, but she's got a passion for fiddling with things which is enough to drive a man mad – I was checking the newspaper returns, and nowadays that's a real headache with hardly a week going by without some fool in Fleet Street coming out on strike about something or other.

I knew he was a detective. I don't mean that I knew the man himself. I didn't. I had never seen him before in my life, but somehow he looked the part, he looked like a go-by-the-rules, stupid official, and of course I was expecting someone.

He produced his card – as required by regulations no doubt. *Det Sgt Wilson, CID Dunsly Police*.

I studied it and did my best to look impressed. Actually I wasn't impressed in the slightest. Or alarmed. I have always despised the police as a thick-witted lot and I didn't doubt for a moment that I would be too clever for them; I found having the sergeant in the shop stimulating more than anything else.

He said he was making enquiries about a murdered woman called Dorothy or Dolly Winter; did I know anything about her?

I told him I had seen the name in the paper, you could hardly help doing so, the *Evening Courier* had been full of it.

'But you never saw the woman herself? This is a photograph of her.'

I studied the photograph long and earnestly; it wasn't a very good one. If that's the best the police can do, I thought, there's not much fear of them catching me. The detective was watching me closely, looking for some sort of reaction on my face I suppose. He didn't get any; just a blank look; but inwardly I was laughing like anything. I was finding all this intensely amusing. I looked at the inadequate photograph – the last time I had seen that harlot's face my hands had been round her neck and I was doing the Lord's work, choking the life out of her.

I didn't, however, propose to tell the detective this and I didn't think that he was likely to find out.

'If she was the sort of woman you tell me she was I wouldn't be likely to know anything of her,' I said, and handed the photograph back.

'She didn't come in here asking you to put a card up?'

I shook my head. 'I don't put up that sort of card in my shop,' I told him. Never have done. I wouldn't do it however much they offered to pay. I suppose they get to know about this so they don't come bothering me.'

He asked Eileen the same question – had she ever seen the woman of the photograph?

Eileen, who can usually be relied upon to do something stupid, couldn't very well say the wrong thing this time because she had been the other side of the town, drinking tea and gossiping with that cousin of hers on the only occasion when Dolly Winter had come into the shop.

The shop is Campbell Hudson, Newsagent, North Street. Only a small business and there's plenty of hard work attached to it what with being at the station early every morning to collect the dailies and never-ending difficulties with delivery boys: but it's a one man affair and that's what I like. I'm a loner. I don't want other people messing me about, offering suggestions, telling me what to do. The Lord tells me what to do and that's good enough for me.

I was able to buy the business because when my aunt died she left me the useful bit of money she had saved up and put away in the Dunsly Building Society. I have always looked on that bit of money my aunt left me as the Lord's way of making up for the bad start I had at home.

It wasn't much of a home. Father was a first-class carpenter, a skilled craftsman, and could earn good money when he was sober. Which wasn't often. I don't know whether he ever wanted to have a son or not; when I did turn up, and as soon as I could understand anything, I understood that I was being laughed at for being undersized.

'Your father's in one of his moods,' mother would say, and I was still only a kid when I realised that father's moods consisted of going down to the pub to get roaring drunk and coming back to beat up everything, including mother. At these times he was dangerous and I used to go and hide in some mangy laurel bushes in the patch at the back of the house that we called the garden.

This highly unsatisfactory man disappeared from the scene, I am glad to say, when I was eleven. Coming back from the pub he was knocked down by a car and died in the ambulance on his way to hospital.

My mother, who had come to fear and hate him and who had to steal from him whenever she could to keep the household going, gave him a splendid funeral – yards of jet black material and no expense spared.

The funeral over and father out of the way, mother then proceeded to go completely to the bad. Looking back on it now I suppose it was a natural sort of reaction; at the time I was only eleven, but an eleven-year-old sees and hears a lot, and somehow understands even more.

36

Very soon the empty gin bottles began to accumulate in the scullery and men were always calling at the house – 'Don't come straight home from school, Campbell, there's a good boy; go round and see your aunt, I shall be entertaining a friend.'

Aunt Mamie. Father's sister. As different from him and from my mother as Cheddar cheese from chalk. There weren't any gin bottles or men calling at Aunt Mamie's house. I know because it wasn't long before I went to live there permanently.

Possibly Juvenile Welfare and the Social Services may have been mixed up in it; but looking back on it I think that it was really the hand of the Lord plucking me out of danger and putting me in the way of salvation.

Whatever it was I was delighted to go.

'Home' for me meant a drunken father for ever tormenting me about being undersized and a mother turning into a prostitute. Compared to that Aunt Mamie's was heaven. And that is the right word to use. At home religion was never even mentioned but Aunt Mamie went to the meetings of the Elect People twice a week and took me with her.

I learnt about the Lord and the work of the Lord and the will of the Lord, and oftentimes it seemed that he was talking to me direct, telling me things he didn't tell to the others, singling me out.

When I was sixteen I got a job at the bookstall on Dunsly station and even then I used to dream about having a business of my own some day, though at the time I didn't see the slightest chance of it ever coming about.

I never forgot being taunted by my father for being undersized, and I thought even if I am small I'll make up for it by being strong so I started going to O'Donovan's gymnasium in Ferse Street two evenings a week for physical training.

So what with the Elect People twice, and often three times, a week and O'Donovan's on Tuesdays and Fridays I had plenty to fill my spare time. I didn't bother about girls. I used to think about them at times and that troubled me a bit, but it was all imagination because at that time I had never been with one, never even kissed one, as I say I didn't bother about them and they didn't bother about me; perhaps they thought, as my father had done, that I was too small to be taken seriously.

It was when I had just turned seventeen that I found myself going to the Elect People evenings (Wednesdays and Saturdays) alone for a time. This was because Aunt Mamie developed some sort of trouble with her back so that walking became difficult. The hall where the Elect People met (the Temple we called it) was at least half a mile away and getting there involved climbing a steep hill.

Naturally Aunt Mamie didn't call in a doctor; she thought all doctors were frauds and taught me to think the same. She relied on a Faith Healer (one of the Elect People) who did a lot of praying and Lord-beseeching but without much effect on Aunt Mamie's back.

One Saturday evening I went to the Temple without Aunt Mamie, which had become the normal thing by then, and because of the storm that was threatening there weren't as many people there as usual. Half way through the meeting the storm began to break. Great peals of rolling thunder that made the tin roof of the place shake. I could see that some of the people were frightened; it didn't frighten me; I liked it; I shut my eyes and hoped that the thunder claps would come louder and louder; they sounded to me like the voice of the Lord.

During the meeting the storm died away rumbling off into the distance and then just at the very end, when we were breaking up, it started again.

Now there was lightning, lovely jagged stuff like the Lord's handwriting in the sky. Everybody began to scurry off homewards as fast as they could, all the women clucking like hens, 'Isn't it awful; just *listen* to it,' and all the rest of it.

Pretty well everybody had come in pairs, but there was

one woman who was on her own, just as I was, and she said she was terrified of going home alone, would I be very kind and escort her? I felt a bit flattered. You don't mind being only five foot four when you are asked to act as escort to somebody.

I had seen this woman at the meetings but had never noticed her particularly and didn't even know her name. Mrs Edwards, she turned out to be, and she had come to the meeting alone because her husband was away on business for the weekend and 'Oh here comes the rain; isn't it awful? We shall both be soaked.'

We were well on the way to being soaked when we reached her front door. By this time I knew her name was Monica and she knew that I lived alone with my aunt and was getting on for eighteen.

'You simply must come in,' she said, 'and dry out a bit, you can't walk home in this rain.'

Inside she lit the gas-fire in the front room and said, 'Dry yourself in front of that whilst I go and get some of these wet clothes off.'

When she came back, only a few minutes later, she had taken off all her wet clothes and hadn't bothered to put on many dry ones; as she moved towards me the long dressing-gown sort of thing she was wearing opened and she had nothing on underneath.

I had never seen a naked woman before and she knew I hadn't.

'I don't suppose you've ever seen anyone like this before, have you darling?' she said – *darling*!

'Come on,' she whispered, 'don't be scared, everything's all right.'

Of course I know now what I ought to have done. I ought to have killed her. It would have been the Lord's work to kill her.

I could have done it easily; my hands were strong enough. Lying on top of her, sickened by the smell and the sweat and the animalism of her ('again, again' she kept sobbing out) I ought to have killed her.

There was a wild delirium in which I hardly knew what was happening and then I rolled away from her, nauseated.

'Darling,' she said, 'wasn't that wonderful?'

'Darling' and 'wonderful' – whore's words, and of course that's what she was, a married whore.

I hurried away from the house, practically running and scarcely knowing whether it was still pelting down with rain or not. I told Aunt Mamie that I had sheltered for a while from the storm and that's why I was so late and I went straight up to my room to change.

I didn't only change. I had a bath. I felt unclean. I hated myself. No more of that, I thought.

Of course I couldn't go to the Elect People meetings any more after that and I had to explain this to Aunt Mamie. Luckily for me her back was still bad and the failure of the Faith Healer to do any good to it had put her somewhat out of concert with the people at the Temple, so when I told her that I felt that the Lord had called me in a special way to do his work on my own she said, 'You leave that lot down there alone, Campbell, and serve the Lord by yourself.'

I was nearly eighteen when I left the Elect People, and for the next six years Aunt Mamie and I used to hold meetings of our own at home. She told me that I prayed better than any of the Temple lot and that the Lord must surely have singled me out.

When I was twenty-four she died and left me her money. It was more than I expected and I realised my chance had come at last. The shop in North Street was advertised for sale in the *Courier* and I bought it. I've been there ever since. Campbell Hudson, newsagent and fancy goods.

When I had been there a year I realised that one person can't run a paper shop on his own. You've either got to employ somebody, in which case bang go all your profits, or you marry and you and your wife do the work between you.

So I married. I married Eileen. As far as I was concerned I wanted somebody to help me run the shop; Eileen, who

40

isn't very bright anyway, was stuffed up with all the usual nonsense about a white wedding and the whole romantic flapdoodle of the business. So possibly we both got what we wanted; I don't know.

Anyway, that was eleven years ago and if there ever was any romance about the affair it withered away long since. I go my way doing the Lord's work in my own fashion and Eileen drinks tea with her cousin and worries about her ridiculous family, but at least she's available to sit behind the counter whenever I want her to.

There has always been this argument about the cards and the magazines. 'All the shops put the girls' cards in,' Eileen says, 'Why shouldn't we?' I tell her that the Lord doesn't want me to have anything to do with that sort of thing and that I never will. Eileen then sulks, she wants to say something rude about the Lord and me but she doesn't dare to. She's afraid of me.

This other business started with Eileen saying one day, 'I think I'll just slip down and have a cup of tea with cousin Connie' – that's the way she talks, 'just slip down'; sometimes I wish she really would slip and break her silly neck.

So with Eileen drinking tea and gossiping with her cousin on the other side of the town, I was alone in the shop.

Alone until the woman came in.

She brought something in with her. An atmosphere. I don't know how to describe it. She had a touch of the gypsy about her. A red, loose, laughing mouth. Laughing at me, I could see that. I suppose she didn't think much of small men.

Usually I don't bother to look twice at a woman. They don't affect me. This one did.

She put the card on the counter and said, 'How much will it be to put that in the case outside? I'd like it there for quite a time. Some months, anyway.'

The card read, 'Attractive energetic young lady gives lessons at home to willing pupils. Tel. 32041.'

'How much?' she asked, 'For six months?'

I shook my head. 'I'm not putting your card up,' I told her. 'I'm not accepting it.'

'Why ever not?'

'Because I don't believe in that sort of thing.'

She burst out laughing. 'Are you one of Mrs Whitehouse's lot?' she asked.

I told her I wasn't one of anybody's lot; the Lord told me what to do and what not to do.

'If he tells you to come up to Wardle Gardens,' she said, 'ring the bell of number 8, ground floor flat. I'm always there.'

When she went out into the street the shop seemed darker somehow and I found I was shaking a little.

When Eileen came back from gossiping with her cousin she wanted to know what had happened in the shop during the afternoon.

'Nothing much,' I told her; naturally I didn't say anything about the woman who looked like a gypsy; the laughing whore who made fun of the Lord.

Exactly a week later the trouble with the tobacco wholesaler cropped up. There's no point in going into all the details of it, but the general position is that small shops like mine depend on a district wholesaler. If anything goes wrong with him you don't get your supplies and you have to disappoint your customers who naturally tend to go somewhere else. When the difficulty started Eileen said, 'Perhaps you had better go up and see him.' It wasn't often that she talked sense, but this *was* sense, and leaving her in charge of the shop I set out for the wholesaler's office in Mancroft Street. Without being sure of its exact position I knew that Mancroft Street was somewhere near the station and in the end I managed to find it all right.

My journey turned out to be unnecessary because the difficulty had already been sorted out and the wholesaler was all apologies and assurances that there wouldn't be any more trouble in the future. I was in no particular hurry to get back to the shop so the fact that the neighbourhood was a bit strange to me didn't worry me in the least; I knew that I was heading in the right direction and that before long I would be back in parts I was familiar with.

I turned a corner and looked up to see the name of the street I was in and there it was – Wardle Gardens.

For a moment the spittle dried in my mouth. I thought, 'The Lord has sent me here; a moment ago I could have turned right instead of left, but something made me turn left and now I knew why it was; now here I am in Wardle Gardens.'

The first certainty came into my mind then with absolute conviction; I knew that I had to go to number eight.

If you never get any messages from the Lord you won't know, you *can't* know, what I am talking about, but to me it was just as though a loud clear voice had spoken inside my head. 'Go to number eight,' it said.

The bell push for the ground floor flat had a little light glowing beside it. I pressed it and waited. When she opened the door and realised who it was she laughed.

'So the Lord told you to come up and see me, did he?' she asked. 'Good for him. I thought he might.'

I didn't say anything. I wasn't going to bandy the Lord's name about with a whore.

'Come on in,' she said.

She was wearing a long, flowing dress, a sort of robe I suppose you would call it, just as the bitch belonging to the Elect People had done.

'Well, now you are here what are you going to do about it, you funny little man?' she said. 'I suppose you've been with a woman before? I'll get you a drink to start you off.'

There were two bottles and some glasses on a side table and she had to bend down a little in front of me to deal with them. For a few seconds she was very close to me, that dark gypsy face, the soft flesh of her neck. . . .

The second certainty came to me then and I knew beyond any doubt what I had to do and I thanked my

43

hours at O'Donovan's for giving me the strong muscular hands to do it.

'You bitch,' I spat the words out at her, for all I knew I shouted them out. I got my hands round that soft neck of hers and she never stood a chance.

Everything was in a mist; a red mist; I did literally see red. The thing I was strangling was the slut from the Elect People who had seduced me; she was all the mercenary whores whose cards I refused to put up; she was all women, all the sweating, stinking femininity in the world. Of course she struggled, her feet drumming on the floor, her hands pulling at mine. I was thankful for them. She didn't struggle much. She wasn't very strong and I was. Only five foot four but strong.

When it was over I didn't feel in the least frightened. The red mist had gone and I was perfectly calm and collected. The Lord had told me to do something and I had done it.

I left her where she was lying, half across a chair, half on the floor, and went to the front door.

Nobody was about in Wardle Gardens so I slipped out, pulled the door quietly behind me and walked quickly away. I walked on air, I was excited and exhilarated, it was a marvellous feeling.

When I got back to the shop Eileen asked if everything was all right now about the tobacco supplies. For a couple of seconds I couldn't think what the silly woman was talking about. The wholesaler and Mancroft Street seemed to be in a completely different world from the exciting one I had just been living in. 'Yes,' I told Eileen, 'everything is settled now.'

I was actually disappointed when there was nothing in the *Courier* that evening. The story didn't come out for a couple of days, which I suppose was a good thing in a way, though I didn't feel in the least frightened. Lots of men must have gone into number eight Wardle Gardens and what was there to connect me with the place.

It came out in the *Courier* that her name was Dolly

Winter and that she had been born in Barwold, a village only a few miles away, where she was going to be buried.

I took a day off and went to the funeral. I thought it was the least I could do. . . .

When Detective Sergeant Wilson asked if I had ever put up a card outside the shop for the murdered woman I told him that that sort of business was against my principles and I never had anything to do with it and I was sorry I couldn't help him.

CHAPTER FOUR

'Will you be staying on for a bit then, Mr Hefferman?' Mrs Dawson asked.

'If it's OK with you, Mrs D.'

Martha Dawson smiled indulgently. She liked this amusing, non-Barwold type male; she didn't know what had brought him to Barwold but if he wanted to go on staying at the Ram it was very much OK with her.

'Or are you going to send me packing?' Hooky asked, feigning apprehension.

Martha Dawson answered that she didn't suppose many women had done that. 'You stay as long as you like, Mr Hefferman,' she added. 'I enjoy our little chats together.'

Enjoyable though they were it was not his little chats across the bar of the Ram which had made Hooky decide to stay on for a while in Barwold. He had come there to do a job but, as not infrequently happened, the job which at a distance had seemed simple enough had turned out, on inspection, to be somewhat more complicated.

With a girl like Tessa Fellingham complications were inevitable, Hooky realised. The Adam's rib business was a mistake from the outset. There everything was, in the morning of time; a lovely sunny garden, no hailstorms, frosts or fogs; all the animals amiable and friendly, no snapping or snarling; and one solitary man, good old Father Adam, strolling around, all on his own, as happy as Larry, with nothing to worry about. A state of things universally, and with every justification, known as Paradise.

Only too often, however, the artist decides to add a final touch which ruins the picture. After six days of strenuous effort the Creator couldn't leave well alone; poor old Adam was put under sedation; operated upon; and a totally fresh dimension was brought into the garden. Discord (surnamed Woman) was born; and to be fair not only Discord but every sort of Delightful and Dangerous Diversion.

Thus ran Hooky's thoughts on the matter and they were abundantly justified by the set-up at Otter Lodge Antiques.

From the first moment they met Tessa Fellingham made it shamelessly clear that she regarded Hooky as being just her sort of man and that the more she saw of him the better she would like it.

On principle Hooky could not claim to object to a certain amount of shamelessness in women, indeed he could recall certain picturesque occasions when it had seemed an admirable trait; but not this time, not here in Barwold. Not with Tessa. This over-energetic, polished little specimen was a shade too hard, a mite too selfish.

The more he saw of the Barwold Antiques set-up the more sympathy and annoyance he felt towards Lynton Hadleigh; sympathy because the agreeable fellow had got himself saddled with a Tartar; annoyance because the ineffectual fool didn't, couldn't and obviously wouldn't get rid of her – at least not until she had got out of him what she wanted, which, Hooky presumed, was his money. Always intensely inquisitive about what made his fellow humans tick, Hooky wondered how it had all begun.

At midday in the bar of the Ram he wanted to ask, how on earth did you let yourself get tied up with all this nonsense, but the question seemed a little crude and he toned it down to, 'I suppose you and Tessa have known one another a long time?'

Tessa herself had gone off on one of what she called her treasure-hunting expeditions and Lynton had been told to look after the shop; but business was slack, non-existent in fact, and he didn't expect Tessa back for hours; he had judged it safe, therefore, to put up the 'Closed' notice and to take himself to the other end of the village to where all his natural instincts led him – the ever welcoming Ram. More than half his reason for going there was the hope of finding there the new acquaintance to whom he had taken an instant liking. 'Tessa's off on one of her treasure hunts,' he explained, 'and I'm not really here at all, I'm minding the shop, so not a word to anyone.'

When the cat's away, Hooky thought smiling, and he felt sympathy for this particular mouse. 'The recommended drink for a non-existent person is a Pimms Number One' he said, 'and Mrs Dawson serves them admirably.'

It was whilst the drinks were being prepared that Hooky asked his toned down question, 'I suppose you and Tessa have known one another a long time?'

'Just over a year, that's all; it's marvellous isn't it? I mean what she's done in the time.'

Hooky thought it was more likely to be a question of whom she had done, but refrained from saying so. He sought enlightenment.

'Well, I mean I'm not much good at organising things,' Lynton went on, 'Never have been, so when old Lucien died—'

'I'm a bit slow-witted,' Hooky warned him, 'so take a sip at your Pimms and shove in a few details about the cast; who is old Lucien?'

'Lucien Hadleigh was my uncle. I used to go and stay with him at Haines, his place in Lincolnshire, in the school holidays when my parents were abroad. And if they weren't abroad they were generally quarrelling, so home was never much of a place to go to; and Haines was a marvellous relief after school term. I was at Harrow. I hated the place. Were you there by any chance?'

'Not quite as bad as that,' Hooky said. 'I was at the other establishment, which incidentally I thoroughly enjoyed, but then as I told you a moment ago, I'm slow-witted, so it just suited me. I seem to remember something about

Lucien Hadleigh – a bit of an eccentric, wasn't he?'

'Lots of people thought he was mad. I didn't think he was mad; I thought he was a jolly decent old boy, and if he wanted to live all by himself in a socking great house in the wilds of Lincolnshire – there were twenty bedrooms in the place and he had something like fourteen cats – why shouldn't he? At any rate he was always jolly decent to me. I must say this Pimms is excellent stuff; I've not often had it before.'

'You're supposed to sip it,' Hooky pointed out.

'That's exactly what I did; I kept sipping at it and it's finished. What about an encore?'

Hooky caught Mrs Dawson's eye and she favoured him with a motherly wink.

'So this decent old uncle of yours handed in his soup plate did he?' Hooky prompted.

The younger man made a grimace of distaste. 'I hate death,' he said. 'Hate talking about it, thinking about it even, it's awful, isn't it?'

'Oh, I don't know,' Hooky said reassuringly. 'Patrimony of a little mould and entail of four planks; it's fair enough, we've all got to come to it.'

'Why? Why can't we go on living?'

> 'Could man be drunk for ever
> With liquor love or fights
> Lief would I rise at morning
> And lief lie down at nights
> But men at whiles are sober
> And think by fits and starts
> And when they think they fasten
> Their hands upon their hearts.'

Hooky pointed out.

Lynton Hadleigh started energetically sipping at his second Pimms.

'You must have done pretty well at Eton to be able to spout out stuff like that,' he said.

'Keeping a quiverful of quotations handy is the easiest

way to appear clever,' Hooky assured him. 'Tell me more about your cat-loving uncle.'

'As it happened I hadn't been to Haines for the best part of two years when the old boy died. I thought he had forgotten me and I was absolutely staggered when the lawyers told me that I had come in for thirty thousand quid and as much of the furniture in the house as I wanted.'

'What about the cats?'

Lynton grinned. 'I can't say I bothered much about the cats. The Inland Revenue sharks proved awkward about the furniture so whilst all that was being sorted out I took the cash.'

'And invested it in some low interest bearing, gilt-edged, safe as houses, dull as ditchwater stock, no doubt.'

'Not exactly.'

'In the good old formula of fast women and show horses?'

'Plus quite a lot of champers. I must admit I made a bit of a fool of myself for a couple of years.'

'Cheer up,' Hooky comforted him. 'The man who has never made a fool of himself will never make anything; and that, if I'm not mistaken, is what they call an aphorism.'

'We didn't go in for those at Harrow.'

'The thirty thousand smackers have vanished, I take it?'

'Into thin air. Long since.'

'Nothing left?'

'Not a sausage. Where does it all go, Hooky?'

'I've often wondered. What happened next?'

'I was just about on my beam ends, wondering where all my friends had suddenly got to, when the legal tangle over the furniture at Haines got settled and I was free to take what I wanted.

'There was a hell of a lot of it – some rubbish, some good stuff – and I had practically made up my mind to have a two-day sale and get rid of everything when I met Tessa at this party. It turned out that she hadn't been invited, but she had heard somehow that I was going to be there and she wanted to meet me; there had been a couple of paras in the gossip columns about the Haines furniture and she was interested.'

Hooky wanted to say 'You astonish me,' but he refrained. There are suckers in every walk of life, he reflected; indeed suckers are an essential part of the economic structure. No suckers, no City of London. He refreshed himself from his Pimms and remained silent.

'Tessa was dead against my idea of a sale,' Lynton Hadleigh went on. 'She had a much better scheme. Why not join forces and set up in the antiques business? My furniture and her brains. I don't know a damn thing about office work or anything like that. She looks after all the money side of things and I give a hand chatting up the customers.'

'And Tessa looks after the books and the money?'

'She does all that. Marvellous isn't it? So here we are in this not particularly lively spot and I must say, Hooky, that coming across you here has been a ray of light in the darkness. Barwold doesn't exactly bubble over with excitement.'

'Folks live here,' Hooky said, 'and where folks live things happen.'

Reflecting, later, on this conversation Hooky's first reaction (in true Hooky fashion) was to congratulate himself on having been so entirely right in his first assessment of the situation. Lieutenant Colonel Henry Fellingham's daughter was the wrong 'un, Lynton Hadleigh was the silly mug. Spider and fly.

To earn his fee all he had to do now was to return to the Smoke and report how matters stood to the Lieutenant Colonel.

Mission accomplished, fee earned.

Yet he hesitated. Where folks live things happen, he had told Lynton Hadleigh in the Ram, earning a look of agreement from Mrs Dawson, who was listening in to their talk at the moment. Throughout his comparatively short, yet colourful, life Hooky had always been plagued by what

51

the Elephant's child suffered from – a 'satiable curiosity; experience had taught him that the actors in the farcical comedy, men and women, are capable of such incredibly silly actions that it was always worth while waiting to see what they would be up to next. What would happen next in the spider and fly situation in Barwold, he wondered; but he knew himself well enough to admit that there was a little more to it than that. The spider might be a wrong 'un, but she was undeniably colourful; if she were less colourful he wouldn't have bothered to stay; he had a hunch somehow that Tessa would provide fireworks before long; he had no idea what form the display would take but he felt sure in his bones that it would take place; that Tessa would be in it, and that there would be something, some odd unexpected little thing, which would point the way to it.

When Tessa came back from her treasure hunting expedition at midday and Lynton asked how she had got on he learnt very little. This was unusual; generally Tessa would return from her forays bubbling over with information about bargains cleverly snapped up or things cannily noted for future reference. On this occasion, however, she was reticent, although there was a gleam in her eye which made her partner think that in due time something would be revealed.

She asked how things had gone at the shop. Lynton reported a dull day and added, as accusingly as he dared, 'Business isn't anything like as good as you thought it was going to be.' He half expected to have his head snapped off for this but, to his relief, Tessa contented herself with saying, 'Oh, well; ups and downs.'

'The mortgage doesn't come down,' Lynton pointed out gloomily. Tessa refused to be pessimistic. 'We might get a stroke of luck any minute,' she said. 'You never know. And by the way, if we go down to the Ram at six-thirty and Hooky is there don't ask him back here for the evening, I've something I want to talk over with you.'

Hooky for his part acted on advice given to him by Mrs

Dawson. When closing time after lunch came she said, in her motherly way, 'It's such a nice afternoon, Mr Hefferman. You ought to walk over to Barwold Great Wood and see the bluebells. A blue carpet they are. A wonderful sight. When you see it all the wickedness in the world doesn't seem to matter so much somehow, not for the moment anyway. It's a great place for young fellows taking their girls; not that you'll be doing anything of that, of course.'

'Mrs Dawson, if you were free and willing who knows what might happen?'

'Go on with you, Mr Hefferman; the things you say! Oh dear, I was free and willing once. Maybe a shade too willing. But we all grow older, don't we? Older and wiser.'

'Older, certainly,' Hooky agreed.

Barwold Great Wood was all of a mile distant and the way there was by unfrequented, traffic-free lanes, often sunk deep between the high, tree-crowned banks. Hooky enjoyed every yard of it; and when he reached them, the bluebells, the shimmering carpet, even exceeded expectations. A magical light indeed, he thought.

The wood was silent, almost uncannily so, and Hooky was disconcerted, on looking up, to find an owl staring fixedly at him from the lower branch of a huge oak. The bird's unblinking eyes seemed to be summing him up, querying what right an intrusive mortal had to be in that silent and secret place.

When he got back to the village Hooky took the short cut through the churchyard which would lead him to the Ram. With rather more than two miles to his credit he was feeling virtuous. He looked forward to recounting his good behaviour to Mrs Dawson and to earning high marks from her for it.

The churchyard of St Thomas the Apostle at Barwold was a neglected place darkened by yews. Unless a service was actually going on the church followed the modern necessity of remaining shut for fear of vandals, and normally the churchyard was deserted.

Hooky was not expecting to see anybody there, but when he was halfway through a figure suddenly caught his eye.

A solitary figure, standing as still as a statue, staring down at a new grave; the grave, as Hooky realised after a moment, of the murdered prostitute who had been buried there recently.

The figure was that of a man; a short man, hardly five foot six in height Hooky guessed, and a man whom he had seen before; the man Tessa had casually told to 'sod off'.

Now he stood there without moving, looking at the grave of the murdered woman, staring down at it steadfastly.

Hooky watched him for a full minute and then went on his way thoughtfully; there was something about that silent, motionless figure which sent a little *frisson* through him. . . .

CHAPTER FIVE

I wasn't surprised when the detective came back to the shop. The Dolly Winter case had been pushed off the front page of the *Courier* by now; if it got mentioned at all it was only in a short paragraph in the middle of the paper to the effect that the police were pursuing enquiries.

This made me laugh when I read it. The truth was, of course, that the police were at a dead loss. Dolly Winter didn't keep any record of the men who visited her and they weren't likely to boast about going there; any one of the prostitute's clients could have killed her and the regulation-bound lot up at the police station had no idea how to find out who it was. But of course they have to put on a show; they have to go through the motions, so they keep asking the same old questions; beating over the same old ground; 'pursuing enquiries'. So, as I say, I wasn't surprised to see him back.

'Sergeant Wilson isn't it?' I said.

'That's right.' He put the card he had begun to show me back into his pocket.

'You came here once before about that woman – I forget her name – who was murdered.'

'Dolly Winter. And I'm here about the same thing again; well, in a general way it's the same thing.'

'Have you found out who did it?'

'We are making enquiries.'

'I don't know what the world is coming to. You can't pick up the paper nowadays without reading about somebody being beaten up or murdered. It makes you wonder what the police are doing.'

'Give us twice the number of men and we could do a lot of things,' the sergeant said a bit stuffily, 'but twice the number of men would mean a sizeable bit on the rates, which isn't a popular idea. The truth is, Mr Hudson, that the public want protection but they don't want to have to pay for it.'

'Quite right,' I agreed dutifully (no sense in getting on the wrong side of them). 'And how can I help you this time, Sergeant?'

'The chief constable wants to tighten up on this prostitute business. He's asking shopkeepers who put up these 'come and get it' cards not to do so without getting the names and addresses of the girls concerned. That would at least give us an idea of the size of the problem and some sort of control of it.'

'I don't put up cards of that sort.'

'I remember you telling me that last time I was here, but I'm going round to ask the shops, just in case. Incidentally, why don't you put up the girls' cards, Mr Hudson? It must mean quite a bit of money in the course of a year.'

'I don't put them up because the Lord doesn't want me to,' I told him.

'Oh,'

He was floored, of course. Bring the name of the Lord into the conversation and people don't know what to do. They're scared. They think you are crackers. You've got them at a disadvantage. You feel infinitely superior to them. I felt sorry for the hide-bound sergeant.

'If any girl does come wanting a card put up I'll get her name and address and tell you,' I promised. 'Meanwhile, I hope you'll find out who did this Dolly Winter business.'

'Like I told you we are actively busy on the case.'

'Any real clues?'

'Something will turn up.'

'Let's hope so,' I said, but of course I didn't hope so and I didn't think so either.

'Who was that?' Eileen asked, coming in from the back.

'A policeman.'

'A policeman?'

'The same one who came before. Asking the same questions. They've nothing better to do; no wonder the rates are what they are.'

Eileen was morbidly intrigued by the Dolly Winter affair; like all unsatisfied women she was fascinated by the whole subject of prostitution and for some days after the Wardle Gardens killing she could hardly talk about anything else.

This put me in a bit of a quandary. I didn't want to seem over-interested in the case, but there was always the danger that if we talked too much about it I might let some remark slip which would sound funny and make Eileen begin to wonder. On the other hand if I appeared unnaturally *un*interested that, too, might look a bit odd.

But, of course, Eileen knew my views about loose women and morality generally and, even if she thought it boring, she believed me when I told her that I didn't want to talk about the sordid case any more. But if I didn't talk about Dolly Winter I thought about her. I'd got to the stage when I was hardly ever thinking of anything else. It wasn't that I was feeling guilty, or having nightmares about what I had done, nothing like that; I had done what the Lord told me to do and what I had done was right. It was simply that I couldn't get the thought of the woman, the idea of her, the remembered picture of her, out of my head. It came into my mind that there must be a reason for this or the Lord wouldn't let it happen; it might be, I thought, that there was something else he wanted me to do. But as I say, I wouldn't say a word to Eileen about Wardle Gardens and I wouldn't let her bring the subject up either. In any case she always had plenty to chatter about, if it wasn't that everlasting family of hers then it would be her other great subject, illness; either an imagined illness of her own, and she had plenty, or a real illness, usually exaggerated, of some acquaintance. When Eileen was talking about illness she was happy, so when the letter came from Marjorie Turner she read it out with obvious pleasure. 'Marjorie Turner has had a heart attack, a bad one,' she announced.

I hardly knew Marjorie Turner, who now lived some eighteen miles away at Heydown, but when she lived in Dunsly she and Eileen had been close friends, gossiping away every day of their lives.

'She wants me to go over and see her,' Eileen said, and waited expectantly.

There used to be a railway station at Heydown and even if getting there on the branch line was a slow business at least you could do it; but the line has long since been closed and as there aren't any buses Heydown is a difficult place to get to. I knew what Eileen was waiting for; she was waiting for me to say I would run her over there in the car. I didn't say it. If she wanted to be taken to Heydown in the car let her ask for it, I thought. I use the car to collect the papers from the station every morning long before most people are up, but after that I don't use it much. I don't like driving and petrol is expensive.

'I suppose you couldn't possibly take me over there,' Eileen had to say at last.

I wasn't enthusiastic, but in the end it was arranged that I would take her to Heydown and she should stay with Marjorie Turner for a night. We had to go on a Wednesday because that was early closing day and the shop shut at one o'clock.

I dropped Eileen at Stone Cottage about half past four. She and Marjorie Turner started gabbling away like magpies at once; if the woman really has had a heart attack, I thought, talking like that will soon finish her off.

I didn't hurry on the way back. There was nothing to hurry for. The shop was closed and it was a lovely sunny afternoon. I had never been to Heydown before and, if I avoided the main road and stuck to lanes, I wasn't any too sure of my exact way back. This didn't worry me, however, as I felt sure that in time I would pick up a road I knew.

After about half an hour something which had been conspicuously absent for a long time came into view – a signpost at a crossroads. The right-hand finger gave me a bit of a shock. It said, 'Barwold 4 m.'

I had forgotten that I was anywhere near Barwold; reading the name suddenly and unexpectedly like that gave me a jolt and started me thinking my Dolly Winter thoughts all over again.

Unconsciously I slowed down and it wasn't at much more than a walking pace that I finally entered the village.

On the day of the funeral I had come to the place by way of footpaths and my first sight of the church had been across the fields, half hidden in the trees; now, coming in the car along a road I didn't know, I found myself suddenly and unexpectedly at the lych gate.

I like the word 'lych'. The death gate, the corpse gate. I stopped the car and got out.

'The Church of St Thomas the Apostle' the notice said, and then the details about baptisms and marriages and funerals and all the rest of the things the parsons charge money for.

I walked throught the lych gate and down the path – which wasn't very well kept – into the churchyard. It wasn't difficult to see where the most recent grave was. I walked over to it.

I stood there for quite a time. I don't know how long, five minutes anyway, maybe more. I'm never in a hurry to leave a churchyard, I like graves and the sense of mortality. And, of course, I liked *this* grave in particular; this was my doing and all the Detective Sergeant Wilsons in the world weren't going to find out the truth about it. I had been too clever for them, and what did they amount to anyway against the Lord?

I stared down at the grave and maybe I even smiled; I was thinking that the Dolly Winters and all the other whores of the world shamelessly putting up their advertisement cards and going about half naked wouldn't have it all their own way as long as I was around to do the work of the Lord.

I walked out of the churchyard feeling quite exhilarated. When I had set out with Eileen the idea of going to Barwold hadn't been in my head; chance had taken me there (was it chance? I wondered) and the visit had excited me.

I drove on slowly into the village proper and when I saw the swinging sign of the Ram I brought the car to a halt in the forecourt of the inn.

I am not what you would call 'a pub man', always in and out of places, but every man, once in a while, feels in the mood to celebrate and in I went.

It was early, not long after opening time, and there was only one other person there. She wasn't half naked this time, she was wearing a sports shirt and trousers. She was sitting on a high stool at the bar showing off her long legs.

She recognised me. I could see that she did. I wondered if she was going to tell me to sod off again. But not this evening; she wasn't in a sod off mood this evening. Maybe she had been drinking; there was a tall glass on the counter in front of her.

'Thank God somebody has come in,' she said. 'I hate drinking alone. I don't know who you are, you funny little man, but I invite you to have a drink with me. Have you ever had a Pimms?'

I could have turned on my heel and walked out of the place. But I didn't. There was something about her, something hypnotic in a way. I stared at her thinking about 'funny little man'; the other whore, the one in Wardle Gardens, had used the same words.

'No,' I answered slowly, 'I've never had a Pimms.'

'I bet there are lots of other things you haven't done,' she said. 'It's never too late to start. Have a Pimms now.'

'Like it?' she asked me when I had taken my first sip of the long drink. Yes, I told her, I liked it.

'I've never known a man who didn't,' she laughed; whore's talk of course, I realised that.

'Where do you live?' she wanted to know. 'In this rather dreary place?'

'Round about,' I told her, 'round about.'

'And are you interested in antiques? I saw you looking at the pieces outside the shop the other day.'

I told her I was interested in a lot of things, in doing the work of the Lord for one thing.

That made her laugh, of course. Her sort always laugh when the name of the Lord is mentioned. She reckoned she had me taped now. As far as she was concerned I was just an undersized little man who had got religion rather badly. She was a lady riding high and wide above everything. She could afford to laugh at me. She wanted to know what I did for a living.

I wasn't telling her that, of course. No fear.

'I mind my own business,' I told her, 'which is more than some other people do seemingly.'

'Hoity-toity,' she said. 'Don't get cross. If you are interested in antiques come into the shop some day; but don't start throwing religious tracts all over the place. I can't stand holy do-gooders.'

The street door opened and in came the tough-looking character I had seen with this same woman once before in this very same place on the day of the funeral. The moment he came in — all six foot of him with broad shoulders to match — I didn't count of course; I was back where I belonged among the lesser breeds.

'Hooky,' she called him, in that infuriating let's-keep-the-strangers-out-of-our-world voice.

I don't know what he really thought of all her high-pitched nonsense, but I guessed he could handle her all right. I think he was used to her sort. He was quite civil to me. He even seemed a bit interested in me. He said 'You were here on the day of the funeral, weren't you?'

'What funeral was that?'

'That girl Dolly Winter who was murdered in Dunsly.'

I shook my head. 'Dolly Winter?' I said, 'I don't know

anything about anyone called Dolly Winter.'

'He goes round doing the work of the Lord,' the woman mocked, 'so you mustn't expect him to know the Dolly Winters of this wicked world,' and she laughed.

I thought they could get on very well without me so I finished my drink and left. As I went out of the door the woman was laughing again. 'All right my beauty,' I thought, 'laugh away whilst you can.'

A fire which gutted a luxury hotel in the country town with every sort of dramatic circumstance, rescuing helicopters and people jumping from blazing bedrooms and the like, was a bit of a godsend to Inspector Marsh. The Dolly Winter murder got pushed even further into the background and now hardly figured in the news at all. No case was ever officially marked 'closed' of course until it was solved; this line was adopted in order to keep up the official theory that the law always got its man in the end. If you believed this theory you could take comfort from it; Inspector Marsh didn't believe it because he knew that it wasn't true; a pretty tough life of combating crime had made him a realist and he didn't think much of his prospects in the Wardle Gardens affair.

All the obvious standard things had been done. The other tenants of number eight – Arthur and Molly James on the first floor and the bed-ridden old lady at the top of the house – had been questioned and re-questioned and their bona-fides checked. Nothing could be found to tie them up in any way with the murdered woman and there didn't seem to be any reason to doubt their statements that they had never been interested in her.

Laborious door-to-door enquiries along Wardle Gardens about men who had been seen going in and out of number eight yielded nothing of any value. A number of people realised what the ground floor flat was being used for and spoke piously of their own rectitude in such matters, but nothing of any practical value had been noticed and nobody wanted to get mixed up in the affair. Their sanctimonious disclaimers caused Sergeant Wilson sardonic amusement. 'You start asking people questions,' he said, 'and you find yourself talking to a lot of saints. Never done a thing wrong in their lives. Wouldn't dream of it. What puzzles me is how all the villainies get committed.'

The tedious question and answer network was widened in an effort to find out something about the murdered woman's associates. The local pub near Wardle Gardens and the local shops where she would be likely to deal were all questioned. A number of people said they recognised her photograph (Marsh believed about half of them), one or two remembered speaking to her, but nothing of any real value emerged. The other known prostitutes in the town were questioned, but all Marsh got from them was a shrill, indignant accusation that pros were rate-paying citizens like everybody else so why didn't they get proper protection from the police instead of harassment all the time.

'The next thing we shall see,' the inspector told Sergeant Wilson, 'is a Prostitutes' Union, affiliated to the TUC most likely; and we shall be stopping people breaking up the picket line.'

Wilson reverted to Wardle Gardens. 'You would think somebody must have heard something,' he said. 'She must have screamed and there would have been quite a bit of noise surely.'

The inspector pulled a dubious face. 'I asked the medico about that,' he said, 'and he told me no, there wouldn't necessarily be much noise; if you're a pretty strong sort of chap, he says, and you know what you are doing, strangling is one of the quickest ways of knocking anybody off; once you stop 'em breathing they don't stand much chance. What about the cards?'

All the paper shops had been visited again and the various proprietors – with the exception of Red Jelf – had promised to get the names and addresses of girls advertising.

Marsh approved of this. 'It's all useful information,' he said, 'and even if it doesn't help today it may come in handy in the future. You never know. My old chief, the one I started under, who caught a lot of villains in his time, always said there was something different about a strangling. If you get one strangling you're sure to get a second,' he used to say.

CHAPTER SIX

'There's a letter for you, Mr Hefferman,' Mrs Dawson said, putting in front of Hooky the large plate containing a rasher of well-cooked bacon, two eggs and a sausage which, admirable woman that she was, she considered a fit and proper start for any man for the day.

Hooky, a poor metropolitan breakfast performer, had discovered that in the countrified Cotswold air he was able to cope with such Gargantuan gastronomic arrangements and he would have fallen to with a will, but the sight of the unopened envelope deterred him.

The handwriting was unmistakable and faintly alarming.

The original address (to Gerrard Mews) had been crossed out by the faithful Roly Watkins who, in readdressing the envelope, had not been able to restrain himself from adding the comment '*oh dear*'. This signified that he, too, had recognised the handwriting and was aware of all it might portend.

Hove

My dear nephew,

Some little time ago an old friend of mine, Harry Fellingham, asked my advice about his daughter. Thank goodness I never had a daughter; I never wanted another woman in the house.

Harry was afraid that his girl was mixing with dubious, possibly criminal, company. I told him that nowadays, with girls going into Fleet Street, the BBC and Parliament, it was very difficult to avoid dubious and criminal company; and that if he wanted to keep an eye on what the girl was really up to he couldn't do better than consult someone who was habitually used to moving in such circles. So I sent him to you. Today Harry told me on the telephone (an instrument which I dislike intensely) that he hasn't yet heard from you.

This may mean that you have run into some unexpected difficulty, or more probably it is just another example of your habitual sloth. It would be interesting to know which.

Your affectionate aunt,
Theresa Page-Foley

A rocket, Hooky told himself, folding the letter away, and a well deserved one. He knew that he should have reported to Henry Fellingham by now and he felt guilty for not having done so.

'I shall be going to London today, Mrs D,' he said.

'You haven't had bad news I hope, Mr Hefferman?'

'A rap over the knuckles from the head mistress.'

'Oh dear.'

Henry Fellingham, who took Hooky to lunch at his Club, was the same well-mannered, sad little man Hooky remembered from their first meeting.

'Barwold, isn't it? She never writes, you see, so I never really know where she is.'

'Yes, Barwold. In the Cotswolds. A pleasant little place.'

'And some sort of antique business?'

'In a house called Otter Lodge. They've got some nice things. This chap Hadleigh inherited quite a bit of furniture from an old uncle living in the wilds somewhere.'

'And what sort is Mr Lynton Hadleigh?'

Hooky hesitated for a moment; he was well aware that crooks come in all shapes and sizes but he didn't think that Lynton Hadleigh was a crook. He said so, adding, 'He's probably a bit of a b.f., but then which of us isn't? A weak character, if you like, but not a dyed-in-the-wool villain.'

'And the business is genuine and straightforward?'

'It's an antiques shop – don't ask too much of it. I wouldn't employ Hadleigh as my financial adviser, supposing I had any finances, but, as I say, I don't think he's a crook.'

'Well, that's something,' Harry Fellingham said. 'That's some consolation for the girl's mother and, poor soul, she needs all she can get.'

Hooky went from the somewhat stuffy proprieties of Lieutenant Colonel Fellingham's Club to the more relaxed surroundings of Gerrard Mews, Soho.

From the Ram in Barwold he had got in touch with a friendly enemy of his in the Yard and had requested certain information. Officially the Yard maintained that all private investigators were a nuisance, if not worse; that they ought not to exist; and that no notice should be taken of them.

Unofficially a certain amount of mutual help was occasionally given – you whisper in my ear and I'll whisper in yours; if you know something that's useful to me I might know something that will help you. It was just such a piece of information, easily obtainable in these computer dominated days, that Hooky was hoping to find waiting for him at Regent House.

'Back from the wilds then?' Roly Watkins greeted him. 'How were the natives?'

'Killing one another occasionally.'

'Must do in order to live,' Roly pointed out. 'The poor old world is getting over-populated. Too many people about. Increase and multiply; He should never have given the order. Time we had another war. Bump some people off and make room for the rest of us.'

'Unless, of course, we happen to be the ones bumped off.'

'Sanfairyan. When it comes we shan't know much about it. One of your back door pals from the Yard has left a message for you; I've got it somewhere.'

A hunt amongst a pile of betting slips brought the message to light. Hooky studied it.

'Campbell Hudson. Newsagent. North Street, Dunsly.'

'Good news?' Roly asked

'Something interesting might come of it.'

'That's what the soldier told the girl,' Roly pointed out, 'and she said she sincerely hoped not.'

After the queer moment when he had seen the little man staring down at Dolly Winter's grave Hooky had walked on thoughtfully, feeling curiously disturbed by what he had seen, until eventually he had arrived at the Ram.

Tessa was there, sitting on her high stool, showing off her long legs, greeting him in that sexy voice of hers. The little man, the grave watcher, was there too. Hooky wondered, with some amusement, what they had been saying to one another, whether Tessa had told him to sod off again and if she had how he had taken it. The little man was invited to have a second Pimms but refused. He exchanged a couple of sentences with Hooky and then left. Through the window Hooky watched him getting into his car.

For someone who didn't know anything about a girl called Dolly Winter, Hooky thought, the man just leaving had shown a remarkable interest in poor Dolly Winter's grave.

'Why on earth are you watching that little twerp?' Tessa wanted to know in amused disdain.

It wasn't so much the little twerp himself that Hooky was looking at as the registration number of the little twerp's car, which he committed to memory.

A request to someone in the Yard who owed him a favour had produced the information which had reached him in Gerrard Mews. Hooky put the message away in his pocket and looked forward to visiting Campbell Hudson the newsagent before long.

Lynton Hadleigh had been given orders not to invite Hooky

back to Otter Lodge because Tessa had something she wanted to discuss, and when the two of them were together he listened with an increasing lack of enthusiasm to what it was.

On the face of it Tessa's latest 'treasure hunt' had not been particularly rewarding. A corner cupboard of poor quality and an undistinguished Victorian what-not had been the extent of her bag.

It was not these that she really wanted to talk about, but she began what she had to say by displaying them. Lynton was not much impressed. 'I suppose we might make a quid or two on them,' he agreed, 'but that's not much use the way things are going – or not going,' he added as a doleful postscript.

Tessa told him sharply not to be so bloody pessimistic. 'If we're hard up we'll borrow,' she said. 'We'll do what everybody else is doing, go to the bank and get a loan.'

'The trouble is,' Lynton pointed out, 'that we've done that twice already and now the bank won't play any more. They say definitely no more loans.'

'Then we've got to think of something else, haven't we?' Tessa said, 'and that's exactly what I've done; I've discovered something else.'

There was a suppressed note of excitement in her voice which Lynton knew of old. She was on to something and didn't intend to let go of it. He waited to hear what it was.

'This place, Wayton, where I got the corner cupboard and the what-not,' Tessa said, 'there's nothing of it. It's scarcely a village, just a few cottages, a scruffy little pub and this one shop. When I left there I thought I'd explore round about a bit, and I got well and truly lost. Talk about Hampton Court maze! It's nothing compared to the lanes round Wayton. Not only no signposts but no houses and nobody seems to live there. Eventually I did come across a house of sorts. Isolated and all on its own. *Pools* it's called.

'The front door was open and an old woman was sitting there. I stopped the car and got out to ask where I was and how the hell I got onto any sort of main road.

'As I got near I could see behind me into the narrow hall and I spotted a decent looking chair standing there. Nothing wonderful but it looked promising. I wanted to get another look at it so when she finished rambling on about how I got back to parts I knew I asked if she would be very kind and get me a glass of water.

'She went into the back parts to get it for me and I took a step inside and began to inspect the chair. I was just coming to the conclusion that I needn't have bothered when one hell of a racket started up in the room on my right. You've never heard such a god-almighty shindy. Terrifying.

'I pushed the door open and went in and there was a cat, a huge yellow and white thing like a tiger, climbing up the side of a parrot cage and the parrot inside screaming blue murder. I pulled the cat off and shoved it out of the front door still spitting and snarling just as the old woman came back with a glass of water as fast as she could, which wasn't very fast; she's got a limp of some sort and gets about slowly.

'She realised what had happened without my telling her and I heard all about how Polly and that wicked Tomkins hated one another; how Tomkins wasn't supposed to go into that particular room but always got in if he could and how grateful she was to me for pulling him off poor Polly's cage.

' "When you came to the door," she said, "I was afraid you were one of those horrible antiques people who come round trying to buy up furniture and things." '

'I told her good lord no. Nothing like that. I had just lost my way. She said it was a good job because there wasn't much in the house anyway and what there was had been left to herself and her sister, now dead, and they had both promised one another not to sell a single item of anything to anybody. "Father left it to us," the old girl said, "and we promised one another never to sell any of it." '

70

'As soon as this rigmarole was finished I asked my way again just to be sure, told her to keep Tomkins away from Polly's cage and cleared out. Pools, the house is called, and now I know how to get there.'

Lynton had listened to this account with a certain amount of interest, but also with growing impatience. It wasn't often that he felt bold enough to tell her so but his opinion of Tessa was that she frequently talked a hell of a lot too much.

'What's the point in going there, then?' he asked, 'if she won't sell anything? And anyway, was the chair valuable?'

'It might be worth twenty-five quid.'

'The bank will be impressed.'

'The chair is nothing. Forget the chair. But in the room where the parrot cage stands I saw four pieces of china. Four Chelsea figures. Now, I know a bit about Chelsea and what's more to the point I know a man in Islington who's mad on the stuff. I didn't have time to examine the figures, of course; not closely anyway, but I got quite a fair look at them and I'm certain they are good. In Islington we could get six hundred, maybe eight hundred each for them, say three thousand for the four.'

'But like I said, what's the point if she won't sell?'

'Who said anything about selling?'

Lynton Hadleigh stared at the smiling girl opposite him and didn't like her smile. He didn't like the way things were going. There were times, and this was one of them, when he wished he had never got mixed up with bossy, ruthless Tessa.

'Who said anything about selling?' Tessa repeated. 'I'm going back to Pools and you're coming with me. You're a friend who's an expert on parrots. You can say you breed the bloody birds if you like. With any luck the old girl will be sitting in the open doorway again. Whilst I'm chatting her up you will be taking an expert's look at the parrot and incidentally swiping the four pieces of Chelsea. You'll have to have a bag of some sort; we'll fix that, and we'll leave the

71

car down the lane a bit, out of sight. Nothing to it. Money for old rope. Three thousand quid for keeping our heads and moving quickly.'

Mrs Dawson was delighted to welcome Hooky back to the Ram. 'I was afraid once you got back to London you might stay there,' she said, 'and I wouldn't have liked that. It's nice having you here, Mr Hefferman, and there's plenty to explore in the countryside, you know.'

Hooky said he was sure of it, and the next day he took the Jag over to Dunsly, parked it at the back of the Regent Cinema and made his way on foot to North Street.

When he reached the shop – Hudson, Newsagent and Tobacconist – he stopped for a couple of minutes to examine the outside of it. There was a glass-fronted case of small ads – repairs carried out in your home; a pram for sale; b & b accommodation urgently needed; a baby sitter wanted for Friday nights; garden work of all kinds and rubbish clearance, reasonable terms – reading through these Hooky was struck by the total absence of a very usual class of advertisement and he wondered why it was.

Inside the shop a woman dealt with his request for cigarettes. Mrs Hudson, he imagined. He treated her to a Hookyesque smile to which Eileen replied nervously. She tended to be scared of men but this one seemed all right somehow.

'Mr Hudson about?' Hooky enquired breezily.

Eileen explained that one of the two delivery boys had not turned up that morning and that Mr Hudson was out repairing the various omissions himself. 'You can't trust anybody these days,' she said.

'It's terrible,' Hooky agreed. 'You've no idea when he'll be back, I suppose?'

Since her husband very seldom bothered to give her any details of his movements Eileen had to confess that no, she had no idea.

'You never know with Mr Hudson,' she said.

72

'I suppose not,' Hooky agreed, 'especially if he has to go as far afield as Barwold.'

The name seemed to surprise Eileen. 'Barwold?' she said. 'Oh, he wouldn't be going there; there's nothing to take him over to Barwold; there's quite enough to do here in Dunsly.'

Hooky said he was sure there was. He picked up his packet of cigarettes and departed wondering why the little newsagent had not troubled to tell his wife about his journey to Barwold to stare at Dolly Winter's grave.

Hooky went into the bar of the Ram rather later than usual that evening. A telephone call to Hove had delayed him. It took him some time to get through and when eventually he did so it was to find himself struggling with an almost impossible line; but all the mechanical squeakings and jibberings in the world could not disguise the high-pitched authoritative voice that answered him, triumphing over them.

'Who is that ringing? You're scarcely audible. Do speak up please.'

'It's Hooky, Aunt Theresa; about Tessa Fellingham.'

'There's no need to shout. Shouting doesn't help on this instrument. About *what* did you say?'

'Tessa Fellingham.'

'That tiresome girl.'

'Well, about her father actually.'

'Do make up your mind, Hooky, I'm in the middle of a rubber of bridge and my partner is displaying all her usual imbecilities so the sooner I get back to the table the better. What about Harry Fellingham?'

'In my opinion the man Tessa is tied up with at the moment is not a crook.'

'I'm sure you would know.'

'So in a way I don't think he's got all that much to worry about.'

'Where human beings are concerned there's always something to worry about. I'm worrying about three no

73

trumps at the moment and about the fact that the sight of an ace and a king together in a hand goes to my partner's head, so I must get back to her. By the way, don't charge Harry Fellingham anything for your services to him, such as they have been; send the bill to me. Harry's got very little money and I've got a lot. Thank you for ringing.'

Hooky put down the telephone refreshed, as always, by contact with the Hove Centre of Asperity and Common Sense. Where human beings were concerned there was always something to worry about – how right the old lady was, he thought; always something to worry and speculate about, which was what gave life its savour.

When he finally reached the bar Hooky was immediately greeted by a telegraphic glance from Mrs Dawson. The place was unusually full and noisy (it was a darts match evening) and under cover of the general hubbub Martha Dawson gave verbal substance to her warning look.

'Mr Hadleigh's here and, oh dear, he is drinking a lot.'

As far as Hooky could see everybody was drinking a lot, something which often happened on a darts match night and to which, in principle, he had no objection; but he respected Mrs Dawson, she kept a motherly eye on her customers and didn't like to see any of them behaving foolishly.

Hooky shouldered his way through the noisy crowd to the far end of the bar where Lynton Hadleigh, catching sight of him, raised a glass in salute. Tessa was nowhere in sight. Off the lead for once, Hooky thought, smiling at Lynton, and making the most of it, well good luck to him. 'Saludos amigo,' he said, 'how's tricks?'

'Thank goodness you've come. I hate drinking alone and with nobody to talk to.'

'Tessa not coming?'

'No, thank goodness.'

'That's not very gallant.'

Hadleigh answered sourly that he was not in a gallant mood. As the evening progressed what mood he was in, and

74

something of the reason for it, gradually became clearer.

It was a revelation punctuated by interruptions owing to Hadleigh's increasingly exhilarated state. At one point, when some dispute arose in the darts match, he volunteered his services as umpire, declaring almost passionately that nobody knew more about the finer points of the game than he did. The bar treated this nonsense with the amused tolerance which Englishmen usually show to a gentleman obviously getting into his cups.

A little later Hadleigh embarked on an elaborate eulogy of Mrs Dawson, the extravagant terms of which made that admirable woman blush a little.

'Now, now, Mr Hadleigh,' she remonstrated, 'you mustn't say things like that.'

Hooky told her to take no notice. 'It's how they go on at Harrow,' he said.

'Oh dear, I thought they were all little gentlemen there.'

'You live in a fantasy world, Mrs D,' Hooky assured her.

Hooky noted what Hadleigh was drinking – a lot of vodka, a little lime and a dash of soda, and wondered how many he had already had; he wanted to ask why gallantry was off the menu that evening, but held his hand feeling pretty certain that in due course in vino veritas would prevail and he would be told.

The vino flowed (vodka and lime) but the veritas was disclosed only slowly and in fragments.

'They're all right of course,' Hadleigh suddenly said after communing with dark thoughts for some time in silence. 'In fact you can't do without them very well, can you? Girls I mean. Women.'

Hooky agreed that a world of He without She would lack a lot of charming variety.

'But there are limits,' Hadleigh went on. 'Of course when I teamed up with Tessa I thought she was bloody wonderful. She *is* bloody wonderful in some ways. But like I say there are limits.'

'Such as?' Hooky prompted gently.

'She's good at this antique lark,' Hadleigh went on. 'She understands it, knows more about it than I do. Mind you, I'm not saying that would be difficult; there's a hell of a lot in the world that I don't know anything about at all. I can sing "Forty years on" but that doesn't really get you very far, does it? When Uncle Lucien died and left me the furniture at Haines it was Tessa's idea to start an antiques shop with it. She said we'd make a fortune. Well, the fortune hasn't turned up yet. In a way it's a bit of a racket really. You pick up a bookcase at some tatty auction for a tenner, do a bit of spit and polish on it and when the right customer comes in, spin a yarn and flog it to him for thirty-five quid. Or fifty if he's a real mug. Fair enough. That's business. Caveat whatever it is.'

'Emptor,' Hooky supplied. 'Caveat emptor, let the buyer beware.'

'Absolutely. Mugs of the world look out. That's one thing; but this other business—'

'What other business?'

Hadleigh pushed his glass across the counter and Mrs Dawson reluctantly replenished it for him.

'It's over the odds,' he went on, 'and I told her so. We had a blazing awful row. She lost her temper as she often does and for once in a way I fairly lost mine. Have you ever hit a woman, Hooky?'

'They're all the better for a good thumping,' Hooky said.

'I nearly hit Tessa this evening. Very nearly. Some day I will. Some day she'll go too far.'

Hooky nodded. He thought it quite likely. Some day she'll tell you to sod off, he thought, just as she told the little man who says he knows nothing about Dolly Winter. . . .

CHAPTER SEVEN

When I started as a delivery boy I used to get ten bob a week and a clip over the ear if I was late any morning, and 'late' meant a minute after six-thirty. If you weren't at the shop by six-thirty, rain or shine, you were late and you heard about it pretty smartly. Nowadays you've got to pay them six or seven pounds, never mind ten bob, and if a boy doesn't feel like turning up on any particular morning that's just too bad – there's nothing much you can do about it.

A delivery boy not turning up means dissatisfied customers – where's my *Telegraph*? How do you expect me to do without my *Times*? What's happened to my *Daily Mail*? and all the rest of it. Everything delivered on the doorstep, that's what people want nowadays, and no allowances made for difficulties with labour and troubles of that sort. So I wasn't in a particularly good mood when I got back to the shop after sorting things out on the round.

I asked, as I always did if I'd been out anywhere, whether anyone had been in. 'Two or three,' Eileen told me, 'trade isn't what it ought to be.' She says that sort of thing with a kind of gloomy satisfaction as though she enjoys saying it. I always feel like telling her that if she would buck her ideas up a bit and be more cheerful when customers came in they'd probably come again. But I've learnt that there isn't much point in saying anything to Eileen; you can't animate a jelly; so I kept quiet, thinking my own thoughts, which is all I want to do nowadays and much more exciting than the chitter-chatter Eileen's so fond of.

But, funnily enough, the next thing she said went straight to the heart of what I was thinking. I hadn't been paying much attention and then that one word jolted me.

'What's that about Barwold?' I asked.

'This man who was asking for you, the one I'm telling you about, he said did you ever get as far afield as Barwold.'

'Barwold? Why should I have any call to go there?'

'That's just what I told him,' Eileen said.

'A customer I suppose,' I said. 'Someone who reckons he knows me,' and Eileen seemed satisfied; she went on talking about something else and naturally I didn't pay any attention to her.

Barwold – there the word was again; nowadays it was very seldom out of my thoughts. I had only to shut my eyes for a moment to see the place. I could see the weed-covered path of the churchyard and the heaped-up grave with the withering flowers on it. Under the flowers and under six feet of earth the whore Dolly Winter where I put her. And then I could see that other whore, the one who told me to sod off, sitting on her high stool at the bar of the Ram, flaunting her long legs, saying 'I don't know who you are you funny little man, but I invite you to have a drink with me.' I couldn't get that woman's face and her high, mocking laugh out of my mind somehow.

Business looked up a bit as the day went on and in the middle of the afternoon a woman came in. I say 'a woman', a girl more properly, she couldn't have been more than eighteen or nineteen.

'I want to put a card in your outside case,' she said, and she handed me what she wanted me to put up. I needn't have bothered to read it to know the sort it was. The usual thing. 'Young lady (blonde) gives private French lessons at home' and then a telephone number.

I remembered what the policeman had asked me to do so I asked, 'What address is it?'

That made her laugh. 'Why, are you interested?' she said. 'It's two Colin Avenue, the basement flat, if you're thinking of coming along.'

I handed the card back to her and told her I wasn't going to put it up.

'Why not?'

'Because I don't want to. I don't like that sort of thing.'

She got quite angry at that.

'It says outside cards displayed for forty pence a week. I want this one displayed for twenty-six weeks and I'm ready to pay for it in advance.'

I shook my head and told her no again.

'I could have you up under the Trades Descriptions Act,' she said.

'Try it,' I told her.

Half an hour later I left Eileen in charge of the shop again and told her I was going out.

'Where are you off to this time?' she wanted to know.

'O'Donovan's,' I said, just to keep her quiet; but I wasn't going to O'Donovan's at all. As a matter of fact I had given up going to the gymnasium in Ferse Street some weeks back. I thought it might be wise.

So it wasn't O'Donovan's I was heading for but the police station; and the beauty of it was that I had a perfectly good excuse and reason for going there. And I wanted to go there. I can't explain it exactly but ever since I killed Dolly Winter I haven't felt in the least afraid of the police. If I've seen a policeman in the street I've felt like brushing against him as I passed. Being near the uniform and knowing that I have completely outwitted them and that they haven't the ghost of a chance of pinning anything on me gives me an excited feeling, a sort of exhilaration, so it was marvellous to have a reason, a good citizen reason, for going down to the station. I couldn't help smiling as I went into the place.

The man at the desk said, 'Good afternoon, can I help

you?' – the usual bureaucratic meaningless greeting. It made me smile more than ever. You can't help me much, I felt like telling him, but I could help you a very great deal if I chose to.

I asked to see Detective Sergeant Wilson: there was some internal telephoning and after a bit the sergeant came down, presumably from his office. He took me into a kind of waiting room, a dusty, cold place, and pretty well repeated what the desk man had said.

'Well, Mr Hudson, what can I do for you?' he asked.

'Nothing,' I told him. 'I'm doing something for you. A girl came into the shop today asking me to put up one of those cards and I got her address like you asked me to. Here it is.'

I had written '2 Colin Avenue' on a half sheet of paper which I passed over to him. He studied it for a full minute as though it might mean something to him; perhaps it did, you never know how corrupt these policemen are; personally, although I know the town pretty well, I had never heard of Colin Avenue.

'Colin Avenue,' he said at length. 'They're setting up everywhere these days.'

'That's because you do nothing to stop them,' I pointed out.

'Prostitution isn't easy to deal with, Mr Hudson; to start with it isn't a crime in itself.'

'It's a sin against the Lord,' I told him, 'and if you let it go on you are hindering the work of the Lord.'

He didn't have any answer to that, of course, so after thirty seconds' silence he asked, 'Did you put this girl's card up?'

'I did not.'

'You're as much against putting up these cards as ever?'

'Just as much. More so, if possible.'

'You didn't ask this girl if she knew the one who was murdered, Dolly Winter?'

'Why should I?'

'These girls on the game often know one another. We want to talk to anyone who knew Dolly Winter.'

'Well, don't ask me. I didn't know her. Have you found out who did it yet?'

'We are working on a number of clues.'

It's a good job you can laugh internally without being heard; 'working on a number of clues' made me roar with laughter inside. The truth was, of course, that they hadn't got a single clue.

'If it's the work of the Lord,' I told Sergeant Wilson, 'you aren't likely to find out, are you?'

Later that day Sergeant Wilson reported to his inspector that the list of names and addresses of accommodating ladies in the town was growing steadily. 'A lot of them we know about already, of course,' he said. 'A new one came in today. Somewhere in Colin Avenue. Hudson, that little chap who won't put up the girls' cards at any price, brought it in.'

'A bit fanatical about it, is he?'

'Very much so. The Lord doesn't like it and Campbell Hudson is the Lord's right hand according to his reckoning.'

'Do you know, Wilson, these religious cranks cause almost as much trouble in the world as straightforward villains.'

'A hell of a lot more if you ask me. You know where you are with a real professional villain. I can get on with his sort; but these the Lord-is-my-master merchants—' The good sergeant shook his head. 'You never know where you are with them, and most of them are anti our lot anyway; the chap who came in today seemed quite pleased that we haven't got anywhere yet in the Wardle Gardens case.'

'Thinking of Dolly Winter,' Inspector Marsh said, 'what's the name of our chap out at Barwold?'

'Police Constable White. Chalky White. He'd never be a Senior Wrangler but he's no fool. He plods along. He's a good copper.'

'Has he come up with anything about strangers recently been seen in the place?'

'Yes. I put him on to that. He's got one character with a bit of interest to him. A chap who's staying at the only pub in the place, the Ram; Hefferman by name. Went up in Chalky's estimation at first because he owns an old Jag and Chalky's mad about vintage cars; then got a black mark from Chalky for being a bit lah-di-dah, one of the now-my-good-man-what-are-you-up-to sort.'

'Any connection with the murdered girl or her family?'

'No, no evidence of that. There's an antique shop in the village, Otter Lodge it's called, run by a couple of these smartie-tartie people who get into antiques these days, half of 'em wrong 'uns if you ask me. Apparently the chap in charge came in for quite a bit of money and went through it pretty quickly; the usual things, women, horses, expensive restaurants and so on; but nothing criminal. He seems to have quietened down a bit now and it's the woman who runs the show. She's out of a good stable, her father's a regular soldier, a Lieutenant Colonel retired now, and by all accounts she's a bit of a high flyer. Chalky says she spends a lot of time in the Ram drinking with this Hefferman character.'

'Do we know anything about Hefferman?'

'Not beyond what I've just said.'

'I think we ought to find out a bit. Do you know any German?'

'German, Inspector?'

'I did a year in Germany as part of my national service. I wouldn't mind living there. I like them. I got on with the lingo too. One bit that I learnt has stuck in my mind ever since – *es ist immer gut etwas zu wissen* – it's always good to know something; you never know when odd bits may come in handy.'

'Shepherd's pie, your favourite,' said Mrs Chalky White.

Police Constable White regarded the heaped-up plate

with anticipatory delight. In the canteen he had the reputation of playing a good knife and fork and he sustained the part nobly at home. With even greater delight he regarded the bottle of beer standing by the well covered plate. Shepherd's pie and a pint of beer. What more could a man ask, especially at the end of a long day.

'That's champion, mother,' he said. 'I can just about do with that.'

Chalky's long day had started with a visit to a farm three miles away to investigate a suspected case of swine fever. Luckily the scare proved false but investigating it took time and immediately afterwards he was called on to deal with some young vandals who were stoning the ducks in the village pond. That matter disposed of he had to visit Knives Farm to tell a very irate farmer that there had been numerous complaints about the mud which his tractor was leaving on the public highway.

'If the stupid people want food to eat they've got to let us farm,' the angry man said, 'not keep on tying us up with every sort of dam' fool red tape regulations. And what about damage done by hikers who never dream of sticking to the footpaths or shutting gates? Why don't you have a go at them for a change?'

Chalky escaped from Knives Farm only to learn that two horses had got out from the next door holding and were running loose on the road. Rounding them up proved a long and tiring business so that when eventually he did get back to his cottage Chalky was more than ready for his shepherd's pie. He had just finished his last mouthful and was turning his eyes expectantly towards a large hunk of Cheddar cheese when Percy Allan appeared.

Chalky knew Percy well, indeed he was known to the whole village, being what Barwold called 'an odds-and-ender'. He did bits of work, mostly gardening, here there and everywhere for people who couldn't manage for themselves.

Percy understood the importance of shepherd's pie and

beer as well as any man did and he was duly apologetic.

'Sorry to trouble you, Chalky, but it's the old lady at Pools.'

Chalky had to think for a moment to a remember exactly where Pools was.

'That bit of a place all by itself?' he said. 'A woman called Clancy, isn't it?'

'That's right. Mrs Clancy. Lives all on her own. A bit queer in the head according to some people.'

'Most people are a bit queer in the head one way or another if you ask me. What about her?'

'She's been mugged.'

Chalky didn't like the word 'mugged'; he reckoned to have a law-abiding patch at Barwold; it was one thing to read about muggings elsewhere, but you didn't expect them in Barwold.

'Mugged?' he queried.

'Well, sort of. It seems a young woman came to the door a day or two back asking her way – she'd lost herself in the lanes round there – and could she have a glass of water. Whilst Mrs Clancy was getting the glass of water her cat jumped onto the cage where her pet parrot is and this young woman pulled it off and shoved it out of doors.

'Then today this same young woman turns up again; how was the parrot and could she have another look at it as she has one of her own and is interested in them. Mrs Clancy says yes, of course she can; and starts to lead the way through the hall. Before she knows what's happening she's had a violent shove in the back which sends her stumbling into the front room, the door is slammed behind her and the key turned in the lock. She says she was pushed so violently that she fell forward and bumped her head on a chair. It probably dazed her a bit. Anyway there she was, locked in her own front room and couldn't get out. She says she did a lot of screaming, and that tired her out and altogether it was over three hours before anybody heard her, and then it was sheer luck, somebody passing by who doesn't normally go that way, and they told me.'

'Is she injured, then?'

'Only this bruise on her forehead where she hit the chair; but of course the old lady is in a dreadful state of nerves.'

'What about the parrot?'

'The parrot's OK; but Mrs Clancy says some bits of china have gone.'

'Bits of china? Valuable?'

'She's doesn't really know. She's had them a long time apparently and she's always imagined they are probably worth a pound or two.'

Chalky sighed. After shepherd's pie and a pint he had been looking forward to dozing in his favourite chair with half an eye on the box, if there was anything worth watching.

'I suppose I'd better go over to Pools,' he said reluctantly.

In due course a report on the incident at Pools reached the inspector's desk in Dunsly and during a routine discussion about all sorts of matters he talked it over with Sergeant Wilson.

'The old girl isn't actually injured, then?'

'Apparently not. Shaken, Chalky White says, but not really injured, beyond a bruise where she fell.'

'Any description of the girl who did it?'

'Young, or youngish. On the tall side. Wearing trousers – jeans I should imagine; and this time wearing dark glasses, which she wasn't doing the first time apparently.'

'Colouring? Eyes? Hair?'

Sergeant Wilson shook his head. 'Nothing reliable. Old Mrs Clancy rambles on and contradicts herself half the time.'

'Any good showing her the rogues' gallery?'

'I doubt it, but we'll try, of course.'

'And the china – what about that?'

'She inherited a few things from her father, whom she describes as a magpie, always picking up odd bits and

85

pieces at farmhouse sales and the like.'

'Was it valuable stuff?'

'She supposes the four pieces must be worth a few pounds each, but as far as she was concerned they were four bits that had to be dusted and no more.'

'What about the car? This girl who came to look at the parrot must have got there by car, presumably?'

'Chalky says Pools is such an isolated spot a car could stand in the lane all day without anybody noticing it; but he's making enquiries, of course.'

CHAPTER EIGHT

The attack on old Mrs Clancy provided the main item of Barwold gossip for not more than a week; other things then claimed attention. A boy was knocked down by a juggernaut lorry in the Square and the big barn at Manor Farm was deliberately set on fire ('arsonized', the *Courier* said), so that the small affair at Pools was forgotten by the majority of people; and this in itself was a commentary on the startling change which had taken place in law-abiding England during the last few years. Not so long ago the invasion of a private house and an attack on an old woman in it would have so shocked the village that nothing else would have been talked about for months; now such incidents were so commonly reported in the papers that nobody bothered much.

PC Chalky White bothered, of course.

The affair brought a certain amount of pressure from his superiors at Dunsly and Chalky didn't like being prodded by those on high, having nobody beneath him to whom he could pass on the prodding process. But even without the 'anything on that Pools job yet?' queries which reached him periodically from Dunsly, Chalky would not have lost interest in the matter.

'Mugged' was the word Percy Allen had used, and it was a word Chalky didn't like, especially in connection with his usually well-behaved patch.

He had made up his mind about one thing from the start – that it hadn't been done by a local. These days the Cotswolds, even quiet by-ways like those round Pools, were so full of cars that you were at the mercy of villains from far and wide. Everyone (which in practice meant just four people) who had been in the neighbourhood of Pools at the relevant time was questioned. Two of them, anxious though they were to have some part in the drama, if any real drama eventually emerged, reluctantly had to acknowledge that they had neither seen nor heard anything.

A third woman thought she remembered seeing a car standing in the lane a little beyond Pools.

'There was a car parked there, was there, Missus?'

'Well, I think there was, Chalky.'

'What time would this be, then?'

'It would be when I was on my way to my sister. The one with the bad leg. I visit her every Thursday. Always at the same time. So I know what time it must have been.'

'And what time was that, then?'

'I'm not quite sure really. I can't remember whether it was there on my way to my sister's or when I was coming back. Silly, isn't it?'

The fourth interviewee, also a woman, was amazed at being questioned. She kept saying indignantly that she had never had anything to do with the police and what would the neighbours think about a uniformed policeman coming into her house and asking questions. She had seen a car, yes, she was certain of that. What sort of a car? She hadn't the slightest idea; she wasn't interested in cars; cars were all very well for people with the money to run them but you couldn't afford a car on the money she got from social security each week; and not everybody got a nice fat pension like the police did.

Chalky ignored the last remark and persevered.

'Was it a big car?'

'Well, big enough, I suppose. What is "big" anyway? It wasn't a lorry.'

'A saloon?'

'I've no idea what the different technical terms are. It was just an ordinary car.'

88

'What colour?'

'It might have been any colour. I didn't notice. I wasn't interested. Blue or red, I suppose; one of those normal colours; or green possibly.'

'Did you happen to notice the registration number?'

'Really! I call this harassment, being questioned like this! Of course I didn't notice the registration number. I don't go about noticing the registration numbers of cars. I shall complain to the Chief Constable if you go on in this way, I shall write a letter to the Dunsly *Courier*.'

Chalky was too old a hand to be upset by any of this, but he had to realise that queries about the villain's car (if indeed the villain had used a car) didn't look like getting him very far; there was, however, another aspect of the affair which might possibly be pursued with more profit, and in any case if he could get some information on the subject head office in Dunsly could hardly fail to be impressed.

Chalky knew nothing whatsoever about the possible value of china figures, and not much (having had very little experience in the matter) of how stolen china might be disposed of, but he didn't see why he shouldn't learn a little about these things; he had never actually heard Inspector Marsh quote his German dictum; but had he done so he would have heartily agreed with it – it was indeed always good to know something.

Beyond noting that they were pretty good customers at the Ram he had not had any contact with the couple who ran the Otter Lodge antiques shop, but Chalky had firmly ingrained in him the maxim in which all old coppers believed – them as never ask any questions never get any answers.

As it happened he had a perfectly good excuse for calling at Otter Lodge; just recently Lynton Hadleigh, who had a weakness for animals, had acquired a dog from a local farmer and the animal had been installed in Otter Lodge, much to the annoyance of Tessa who considered it a damned nuisance.

Chalky had long been of the opinion that the ridiculous 37½p dog licence should either be put up to something worth while, say at least five pounds, or better still abolished altogether, and worrying about who had, or had not, paid their dog licence fee came very low on his list of priorities.

But occasionally, as now, it provided a convenient excuse.

The sight of the blue uniform approaching the front door quickened Tessa's heartbeat slightly but it didn't cause her any sort of panic. It gave her the same sort of feeling she experienced when going out hunting; it put an edge on things. As yet she had not met PC White, but PC White was a man and she had no doubt she could handle him.

When she opened the door to admit him, she was giving her best performance – smiling, open-mannered and extremely attractive.

'Mr White, isn't it?' she asked.

'That's right.' Chalky didn't know whether to add 'madam' or 'miss' and in the end said neither.

Tessa smiled at him. 'I do hope you've come as a customer, Mr White,' she said, 'and not because we've committed some dreadful crime.'

'Nothing to do with crime,' Chalky assured her, 'but I see you've got a dog recently and I was wondering if you had remembered to get a licence for it.'

'A licence? Good God, we don't have to pay to keep the beastly animal, do we?'

'I'm afraid you do,' Chalky told her, 'and people often forget, so I like to remind them to prevent them getting into trouble, especially as it's such a small amount, only thirty-seven and a half pence.'

'Thirty-seven and a half p.! – it's a damn fool amount. Can I give it you now?'

'Not me. At the post office. Any time it's convenient; no hurry so long as you remember.'

'Well it's jolly nice of you to come round and remind us,' Tessa said. 'I was just about to have a glass of sherry, will you join me? I'm sure you ought to say no you can't, you're on duty; but now you've told me about the dog licence the duty part's over, isn't it, and you can relax, surely?'

'That's very kind of you, Madam,' Chalky said. 'I should like that.'

'A glass of sherry in the middle of the morning never did anybody any harm,' Tessa said, pouring out two generous schooners and handing one to Chalky. 'I'm sure you're called Chalky, aren't you?'

'That's right, Miss. All Clarkes are Nobbies, all Whites are Chalkies; that's what everybody calls me, Chalky.'

Chalky didn't often drink sherry and he liked the comforting taste of it. He felt encouraged to go on to the real purpose of his visit.

'A bad business about the old lady at Pools,' he said.

Tessa put on her sympathetically interested air, a pose which she could assume convincingly.

'I saw something about it in the *Courier*,' she said, 'Beaten up was she?'

'Not exactly beaten up; in fact she wasn't seriously hurt at all; just scared.'

'And there was something about a parrot, wasn't there? Was it stolen?'

'The parrot wasn't stolen, but four pieces of china were.'

'China? Cups, saucers, plates – that sort of thing?'

'Figures more, the old lady says; four china figures. They'd be valuable, I suppose?'

Tessa burst out laughing. 'Good heavens, don't ask me. I know nothing whatever about china. We never touch it here. As you can see,' she embraced the shop with a gesture, 'it's all furniture with us. Heaven knows what the old lady had in her cottage, it might have been valuable, it might have been rubbish; she probably doesn't know herself – does she?'

'I don't think she does,' Chalky confessed. 'She says the

91

four bits might be worth a pound or two.'

'Well, there you are, if you go down to the Lanes in Brighton you'll find hundreds of bits of china worth a pound or two.'

'The Lanes in Brighton – is that where whoever stole them would get rid of them?'

Again Tessa laughed heartily. 'God knows,' she said. 'Getting rid of stolen china isn't my line, selling genuine antique furniture is. Will you ever find out who did it?'

In the whole area under Inspector Marks's supervision the detection rate of crime was 31 per cent, which is to say that in every hundred cases reported to the police the villain got away scot free sixty-nine times, thus putting in serious doubt the validity of the comforting statement that crime doesn't pay.

PC White was aware of this statistic, but he saw no point in retailing it to a member of the public, however sympathetic and helpful she was turning out to be.

'We never like to say we're beaten,' he said, 'but a case like this isn't easy.'

Tessa said she was sure it wasn't. 'Have another sherry?' she added.

Chalky refused a second sherry. He said he had very much enjoyed his one glass and the matter of the dog licence wouldn't be forgotten, would it?

'I'll rustle up thirty-seven and a half p. from somewhere and go down to the post office this afternoon,' Tessa promised.

'And, of course, if you should hear anything about the bits of china—'

Tessa nodded. 'I don't think I'm likely to,' she said, 'but if I do, you can rely on me.'

Chalky went away from Otter Lodge warmed by a glass of good quality sherry and by the agreeable feeling of having done something which ought to earn him a good mark with the high-ups at Dunsly. At least he could now talk about the Lanes at Brighton, though what good that would be without a description of the china figures he didn't know, and so far old Mrs Clancy, who hadn't really looked at the figures for years, had given only sketchy and contradictory accounts of them.

As soon as the blue uniform was off the premises Tessa treated herself to a second glass of sherry which she considered had been thoroughly well earned.

She didn't know about the 69 per cent unsolved crime statistic but common sense told her that an in-and-out job like the one she had carried out at Pools must be very hard for the police to do anything about: no fingerprints (she had been wearing gloves), no proper description (she was wearing dark glasses and with any luck the old woman would be too scared), and the car not spotted, tucked away in a little-used lane.

The programme now, therefore, was to lie low for a bit; let the police go ferreting about in the Brighton Lanes as much as they liked; then in due time get in touch with the fanatical collector of Chelsea in Islington and pick up the cash.

When she had first suggested the Pools job to Lynton he had unexpectedly turned it down; thinking things over, she had realised that his refusal wasn't altogether unexpected. 'Lynton just hasn't the guts,' she thought, 'no good putting him up on a horse in a point-to-point, he'd never face the jumps.' So to her extreme satisfaction she had carried out the raid on Pools entirely alone, without anybody else knowing anything about it. But Lynton would have to be told and she was looking foward to telling him. He had been despatched to the village to do some shopping and when he got back he asked, 'Wasn't that the bobby I saw coming away from the shop?'

'It was.'

'What did he want?'

'Thirty-seven and a half p.'

'Thirty-seven and a half p.? Whatever for?'

'For a licence for that damned dog of yours.'

'Oh Lord, I'd completely forgotten about a licence.'

'We didn't want the animal in the first place.'

'Well, I wanted him and I'll fix the licence business, so don't turn nasty over that. Was that all the bobby came about?'

'It wasn't all we talked about, anyway.'

'What else?'

'He's called Chalky and I gave him a glass of sherry.'

Lynton laughed; he approved of that. 'Stand the Law a drink whenever possible,' he said, 'can't go wrong there.'

'And, of course, we talked about the china.'

'What china?'

'Oh, grow up, Lynton, be your age; what china do you think?'

Hadleigh stared hard at her, hating that taunting smile of hers.

'It was you who did that job at Pools,' he said at last.

Tessa nodded and her smile increased. She could see that he was getting angry and she didn't mind his getting angry, she was enjoying herself.

'Tell me,' he said quietly.

'Tell you what?'

'Don't be so bloody clever, Tessa,' he exploded. 'I want to know what you've done, what happened.'

'Didn't you read the account in the *Courier*? One of these dreadful tearaway young villains locked the old girl up and lifted four pieces of china.'

'A tearaway young villain?'

'That's what the police think – I hope.'

'And where are the china figures now?'

'In this building. I've hidden them. They're Chelsea and they're good. In time we'll get quite a lot of money for them.'

Hadleigh crossed to the drinks cupboard and helped himself generously. The girl watched him in amused contempt which she didn't bother to disguise.

'Don't get fuddled just because you're scared,' she said.

'We've only got to keep our heads and we'll get enough cash to pay off all we owe.'

Hadleigh shook his head. 'I don't want to get mixed up in this,' he said. 'I don't want to do it.'

'The trouble with you, Lynton, is that you haven't got the guts to do it, you haven't got the stomach for it. You had better content yourself with getting the dog licence and taking the stupid animal out for a walk.'

'You look flustered, Mrs D,' Hooky said, 'what's troubling you?'

'Oh dear, there's always something, Mr Hefferman, isn't there?'

'The eternal pattern of the carpet of life is full of repetitive and annoying intricacies,' Hooky pointed out.

Mrs Dawson said, a little huffily, that she was sure anyone must be very clever to say things like that but it didn't help much, did it?

Feeling slightly chastened Hooky hurriedly added, 'I didn't say it, Mrs D, don't blame me; a Chinaman called Lu Wang said it about two thousand years ago.'

'I suppose the Chinese have their worries, like the rest of us.'

'What's worrying you, Mrs D?'

'It's Lucy. She must get back because of the boys.'

Mrs Dawson's married sister had been on a two day visit to the Ram and was due to be taken back home, some fifteen miles away, that afternoon, but George Dawson's car, much to his astonishment, obstinately refused to show a spark of life.

'Never known such a thing,' George kept repeating, 'never. It's never done this before.'

'Well, it's done it now,' his mother pointed out sharply, 'so how are we going to get Lucy back? And go back she must because of the children.'

George, an admirable fellow in many ways but not much use in any sort of a crisis, didn't know how they were going

95

to get Lucy back, and it was left to Hooky, when he heard of the difficulty, to come to the rescue.

At three o'clock in the afternoon, therefore, Lucy was tucked into the passenger seat of the Jag and declared that she had never felt more ladylike in her life. 'It's one of these advantage cars isn't it?' she said. 'I never thought I'd be sitting in one.'

Lucy was safely delivered home where Hooky politely but firmly declined an invitation to stay for family high tea. His passenger had talked non-stop all through the journey and would obviously go on doing so during tea.

It was a relief to be alone in the Jag again ambling gently back through the Cotswold lanes. There was no reason to hurry and Hooky didn't hurry. There was no reason to think of anything in particular and Hooky let his mind wander over many things – he thought of Roly Watkins faithfully holding the fort in Gerrard Mews and he half wished he was back there in the petrol fumes and the grime and the urgency of the Great Wen with him; he thought of the Lady Macbeths of life and of how troublesome they must be to their husbands; he thought of Lucy's ceaseless flow of chatter and rejoiced at having escaped from it; he thought what a bore it was, even when not in any hurry, to come round a bend in a narrow lane and find oneself penned behind a small, very un-Jag-like jalopy that couldn't be passed because of the narrowness of the lane.

The lane forked; the jalopy went one way, and in order to have the road to himself again Hooky went the other. Fifty yards later there was a click in his brain. Following the little space-denying car he had been idly reading its number plate without any special interest and now, suddenly, he realised that it was already known to him. He had noted it once before and had made enquiries about it.

Now his thoughts became considerably more practical, wondering what the puritanical little newsagent of Dunsly was doing once more in the neighbourhood of Barwold, the place which his wife declared to be right outside his beat. Had he come, Hooky wondered, to stare down again at the grave of the strangled prostitute, and if so why?

He had set out on the business of taking Lucy home in an easy, relaxed frame of mind, content to shut his ears to the unending flow of truth and to think how lovely the Cotswold lanes looked and how splendidly his faithful old Jag purred along; but now a cloud, like the proverbial man's hand, began to loom on the horizon of consciousness; Campbell Hudson, newsagent and prostitute hater, was becoming something of a problem in Hooky's overactive brain.

These thoughts, indefinite yet vaguely distressing, were still occupying him when he got back to the Ram and taking a duster from the glove box began lovingly, and quite unnecessarily, to rub up the metal work of the Jag.

He was thus employed when Lynton Hadleigh, passing by the entrance to the inn yard, saw who was there and came in accompanied by a small brown and white dog. Taking a quick glance at him Hooky was alarmed; he didn't like the look of this bird at all.

'Too early for a noggin, sport,' he said, 'the Ram keeps strictly legal hours.'

Hadleigh said he didn't want a drink. 'I've been tight once today already,' he said, 'and that's enough.'

'Absolutely,' Hooky agreed. 'Nothing exceeds like excess.'

'Polishing up the old bus?'

'Taking some of your Cotswold dust off her. Nice little dog you've got.'

'Midge.'

Hooky had a soft spot for all dogs and he and Midge communed for a few seconds in amiable pourparlers.

'You have to pay thirty-seven and a half pence for a dog licence, did you know that?' Hadleigh said, 'and some people object to paying it.'

The remark meant something, Hooky realised, and he

wondered what the hell it was. 'Some people would object to anything,' he pointed out philosophically.

Hadleigh nodded. 'There are things I object to,' he said. 'Lot's of things I don't care about but some things I do, enough is enough, so far and no further. I said all this to you once before, didn't I?'

'Something like it, sport, something like it. But don't worry, repetition is good for the soul. How's business? Flourishing? Lots of suckers paying over the odds for old corner cupboards and the like?'

'I wish I'd never been persuaded to go into the antiques business,' Hadleigh said. 'I wish I'd never let her talk me into it.'

'Things a bit tricky at times, are they?' Hooky ventured to ask.

'But, like I say, there are limits.'

'Absolutely.'

'When she said she'd have Midge put down because she couldn't stand him yapping and he wasn't worth the thirty-seven and a half p. licence, that's what finally made me see red.'

Duster in hand, Hooky stepped back to admire his gleaming handiwork and became aware of an audience. PC White stood at the entrance to the inn yard. Had been standing there for how long, Hooky wondered.

'Smartening it up a bit then?' Chalky White said, 'that's the idea.'

CHAPTER NINE

Before the business in Wardle Gardens I hardly ever dreamt. I have to be up early every morning (just after four-thirty) because of getting the papers from the station, so I've got into the habit of going to bed directly after the headlines of the nine o'clock news, and as soon as I'm in bed I'm asleep, and then, as I say, I hardly ever dream.

Aunt Mamie was a great dreamer and a great believer in dreams. 'The Lord speaks to us in dreams,' she used to say, and if she had a dream which she didn't understand, or which frightened her (and she was very easily scared) she would be unhappy for days. 'What do you suppose it means, Campbell?' she would ask, and I used to say that the Lord would tell me what it meant in good time and meanwhile not to worry.

It was after going to the whore's funeral that I began to dream. What I dreamt about was Barwold, the place; especially the churchyard. I had only to put my head on the pillow and I could see the dark yews and the headstones of the graves and the heaped up mound that as yet had no headstone. But I didn't dream about the girl Dolly Winter. When I stood (in my dream) staring down at the grave it wasn't her face that I saw but another one – the face of the tall woman who found my lack of height so laughable; who asked, 'Have you ever had a Pimms?'; who said, 'I bet there are lots of things you haven't done, but it's never too late to start'; the high-class, well-bred whore.

When I thought of Barwold I thought of her; and when I thought of her I thought of Barwold.

The name kept echoing in my head; at times I was attracted by it, at times scared, and it occurred to me that I hadn't been half inquisitive enough questioning Eileen about the man who had come into the shop when she was in charge saying something about did I ever get as far afield as Barwold. At the time I had thought it was just some casual query, lots of people come into a shop, even a small shop like mine, and they all reckon to know the shopkeeper – more people know Tom Fool than Tom Fool knows as the saying is – but thinking back to the visit of this man, whoever he was, I wondered why Barwold? What had he to do with the place? And why should he think that I had anything to do with it?

'That man who came in the other day,' I said, 'when I was out.'

'What man?' Eileen asked. 'You are always going off to different places nowadays, I never know where, leaving me to look after everything, and lots of customers come in. What man?'

'The one who asked did I ever get as far afield as Barwold.'

'Well, you don't, do you? Or at any rate if you do you don't tell me about it. But then, of course, you never do tell me anything, do you?'

When she was in a bad mood – and I could see that for some reason she was in a particularly bad mood that evening – this was one of her favourite complaints, that I never told her anything. Well, of course I didn't. I couldn't be bothered to. What went on in my head was between me and the Lord, it was much too private and exciting to be shared with her.

'What sort of a chap was he?' I asked.

'What sort of a chap?' Eileen laughed in the way she does when she has plucked up the courage to say something nasty. 'He was tall and well built, that's what he was.' Of course this was a sneer at my five foot four, which she ought to have got used to by now. I let it pass; I didn't want a quarrel, I wanted to find out something, or more correctly I wanted to reassure myself that there wasn't anything to find out.

'And what had he got to do with Barwold?' I asked.

'How should I know? And anyway what's so special about Barwold?'

I began to think that I might have made a mistake in bringing the subject up at all.

'There's nothing special about Barwold,' I told her.

'*Do* you go there? Have you ever been there?'

'Why should I?'

Eileen laughed. She was enjoying herself. It wasn't often that she felt brave enough to tackle me like this and she was enjoying it. 'What do I know about why you do things?' she asked. You never tell me anything. You might have some woman there for all I know.'

Eileen and I had long since given up sharing the same bedroom and we never by any chance discussed sexual matters together so, in a way, this unexpected remark of hers shook me. But then again, in another way, it was hideously true. There *was* a woman in Barwold, the whore with the long legs and the contemptuous laugh, the whore whom I couldn't get out of my mind.

Suddenly my thoughts were jerked back to something I hadn't consciously thought about for a long time – the night of the meeting of the Elect People; the storm and the woman who had asked me to escort her home and had seduced me; '*I don't suppose you've ever seen anyone like this before, have you darling?*' – darling!

'Well, why don't you answer about having a woman at Barwold?' Eileen asked.

'Because it's such a stupid question,' I told her, 'and you ought never to have asked it.'

'Oh no, of course not. We're none of us human, are we? The way you and I go on, or don't go on, we might as well not be human. Or are you thinking that I tried to get into conversation with this man who talked about Barwold?'

'You might have done.'

'I suppose you think I try to get talking with every man who comes into the shop.'

'I didn't say that. I didn't say anything like that.'

'You never say anything, that's the trouble. You don't think people are worth saying things to. You don't think people have feelings. You're not interested in human beings. It's the Lord this and the Lord that all the time with you. You want to forget the Lord and think about human beings for a change. The only reason you married me was to get someone to look after the shop. Someone you didn't have to pay.'

If she hadn't dragged in the name of the Lord like that I might have felt some sympathy for her. What she said about my marrying her was absolutely true, of course. But, after all, what had she got to grumble about? We have a comfortable home. No luxuries certainly, but I don't like luxury. But we never go short of anything. On two afternoons a week she 'slipped down' to that cousin of hers for tea and gossip. About me and my inadequacy as a husband very likely. Once a week the two of them go off to Bingo. I never interfere with any of this. She goes her way and I go mine.

The point is that her way doesn't matter and mine does. She sneers at the Lord. No doubt she and her cousin laugh together about me and the Lord. Let them laugh – the crackling of thorns under the pot. I lie awake night after night, listening to what the Lord tells me to do and wondering what he will lay on me next.

'Tall and well built,' Eileen had said, so I thought it might have been the chap I had heard them call 'Hooky' in the Ram in Barwold. We had exchanged a certain amount of talk and he had always been civil; in fact, in spite of his being on friendly terms with the whore, I rather liked him. But I had been careful not to tell any of them up there my name, or to say anything about the shop; so how had he come to find out anything about me? And why?

I kept these thoughts in my head for a couple of days, turning them over again and again. Sometimes I could almost persuade myself that it was pure chance that someone had come in and spoken about Barwold. But I never quite believed that. The more I see of things the less I believe in pure chance. I don't think the Lord works that way. I think there's a reason behind everything, that it all fits into a plan.

One day the policeman, Detective Sergeant Wilson, came into the shop again. I wasn't scared, but all the same I wished he hadn't come. The less I saw of the police, and they of me, the better; but, as I say, I wasn't scared; they had nothing on me and they weren't going to get anything on me.

This time Sergeant Wilson started by buying a packet of cigarettes. Maybe he really wanted them, maybe it was just his way of breaking the ice; of getting on friendly terms, of leading up to something.

'How's business?' he asked.

'So so. Mustn't grumble.'

'Any more young ladies with cards?'

'I don't call them young ladies,' I told him. 'I call them what they are, prostitutes.'

'You're quite right, of course, Mr Hudson. Any more pros with cards, then?'

'No. The word gets round that I won't put their cards up here so for the most part they don't try.'

I thought it would look more natural to show a little curiosity than not to show it so I carried the war into his camp and asked, 'How's that business in Wardle Gardens coming along? Have you found out who did it yet?'

'We're working away at it,' Sergeant Wilson said. 'We'll get a line to follow in time, and meanwhile, of course, we're anxious to talk with anybody who knew the murdered woman, that's really why I'm here this morning. I'm going round all the paper shops again saying if a girl comes in wanting a card put up chat her up a bit and try to find out if

103

she knew Dolly Winter, and if she did, tell us. Will you do that, Mr Hudson?'

'Of course,' I told him. 'I'll do anything to help.'

Then a strange thing happened, something which, thinking about it afterwards, I found disturbing, and even frightening. I had a sudden compulsion to say the word *Barwold*. I had to say it. I had to say it in front of this policeman. You can call it a kind of bravado if you like; or you can say it was part of the pattern, destiny working itself out. I don't know what it was, but the name of that place was burning in my brain and it had to come out. I had to pronounce it.

'Let's see,' I said, as off-hand as I could, 'wasn't she buried in a place called Barwold?'

'That's right. That's where she came from. She was born there. Barwold. Do you know it?'

'I don't know it, but I think I've been through it once and the name stuck.'

'It's not much of a place. Nothing to it really. She's buried in the churchyard there. One of these untidy, ill-kept places; they give me the creeps.'

'Me too,' I lied cheerfully, 'but I suppose we shall all get there in time.'

As soon as the sergeant had gone Eileen came in from the little back room where, if she lived up to form, she must have been trying to listen in to what we were saying, but probably without much success.

'What did he want?' she asked.

'A packet of cigarettes,' I told her.

'And what were you talking about all the time, then?'

'Mortality.'

Mortality was what I told her; but I very nearly said 'Barwold'. That's what I would have liked to tell her. I would have liked to say we were talking about the place which excites your stupid curiosity and about which I shall never, in fact, tell you anything, that's what we were talking about. That's what it would have been truthful to tell her,

104

because *Barwold* was the one word which stayed with me from Sergeant Wilson's visit.

Not much of a place, he had said, and the churchyard gave him the creeps. It didn't give me the creeps, it excited me. Just as Barwold itself excited me. I must go there again, I thought, and find out about this man Hooky, find out if he did come in here asking about me; but at the back of my mind I knew that the real reason why I had to go back there wasn't to see this Hooky person; it wasn't a man; it was a woman.

Eileen's complaint that I never told her where I was going was justified, of course. I had got into the habit of saying, 'I'll be back in an hour or two, keep an eye on things whilst I'm away,' and off I'd go. Possibly for the two hours I spoke about, possibly more. She soon discovered that it was a waste of time trying to find out where I'd been so she gave up trying. As I've tried to explain, this didn't mean I had secret assignations or anything like that, very often all I did when I left the shop was to walk the streets of Dunsly noting all the vulgarity and wickedness of the world and waiting for the Lord to give me something to do; it was just that talking anything over with Eileen, discussing anything with her, didn't seem worth while. It was what the Family Advice people (if I had ever been fool enough to go to them) would have called 'a failure of communication' – I didn't communicate with Eileen, I communicated with the Lord.

So normally if I felt like going out I went out and didn't bother to give any explanation or reason. But suddenly with this Barwold business things had become a little different. Or maybe I was getting scared and just thought they were different. Anyway, there it was, Eileen had got hold of the name Barwold and it had evidently lodged in her suspicious little mind so I thought it would be wise to be more careful about my comings and goings for a while.

So when the special meeting of local newsagents was called I told Eileen something about it and explained that I would have to attend. What we were going to talk about was Sunday trading; the local Council, a pretty unintelligent lot, wanted to restrict us to Sunday papers and nothing else; most of the shopmen wanted to be able to sell anything; personally I would have been happier not to open on a Sunday at all.

There was only a handful of us and the thrusting little chap who had more or less appointed himself as chairman had managed to persuade the local MP to meet us and listen to what we had to say. Hence the meeting.

'I don't suppose anything will really be decided,' I told Eileen, 'but we will probably be all day talking about it, so expect me back when you see me.'

This was what I genuinely thought would happen, but actually things turned out differently.

To start with the chairman was late, which was unlike him as he is normally over fussy about time and punctuality. When he did eventually appear he was in a bit of a fluster. He was late, he explained, because at the last minute there had been a telephone call from the MP saying that urgent Government business had cropped up and he wouldn't be able to come to Dunsly after all; followed, of course, by a whole rigmarole of apologies and regrets and good wishes which must have made it an expensive call which no doubt the taxpayer would ultimately pay for.

So there it was – no MP and therefore no real person for a meeting.

The others seemed disposed to stay on for a while and discuss things amongst themselves; I said I thought I had better be getting back. I didn't go back. There was no particular reason why I should. Eileen wasn't expecting me and business had been so slack lately she could manage perfectly well on her own. I found myself with an unexpected day off. A free day.

Except, of course, that I wasn't a free man.

When I was telling them at the meeting, 'In that case I think I had better go back,' even as I was saying it I knew perfectly well what I was really going to do.

I was going to Barwold. I realised it was a heaven-sent opportunity. Even if the news that the MP hadn't turned up came out and Eileen read about it, it would be easy to tell her that we had sat on and talked things over among ourselves.

I had taken the car to go to the meeting, which was unusual for me because normally for any business in the town I go on foot, but on that particular day, by chance, I had decided to take the car. And suddenly I wondered if it *was* just chance, or whether it was part of the pattern. If I had had to go back to the shop to get the car I would have had to explain things to Eileen; as it was the car was standing outside the room where the meeting had been arranged, and all I had to do was to get into it and drive off.

It would be impossible to explain why it had suddenly come into my head that I had to go to Barwold. Except, of course, it wasn't sudden. The name of the place, the memory of the place, the darkness of the tree-shaded churchyard, the woman sitting up at the bar laughing at me – these things were in my mind all the time, underlying all my thoughts, they were images that never left me.

The meeting which never took place had been fixed for eleven-thirty. What with the chairman being late and the discussion that followed his eventual arrival time had gone on a bit and it was half past twelve or maybe a shade later when I started to drive away.

I wasn't in any hurry, and in a way that was strange seeing that I was under a compulsion. I had to go to Barwold. I knew that I had to go there. We don't do much by chance in this world. There's a plot; somebody writes that plot; we are given our parts in it. And it was precisely because I had no doubt at all that I had to do what I was doing that I wasn't in any particular hurry about it. The inevitable inevitably happens.

When I was halfway there I pulled into the forecourt of a country inn. The Seven Stars I think it was called. Not so

107

long ago it would probably have been a beer house, now it was tarted up no end and advertised Pub Grub. Food at the Bar. Fresh cut sandwiches. Chicken in the Basket, and all the rest of it.

It was comfortable enough inside and it wasn't crowded. When the barman asked me what I wanted I had a wild temptation to say 'a Pimms please'; but of course I didn't; I ordered my usual half pint of bitter and said I would like a ham sandwich, and then went to sit down by the window.

The girl who presently brought me my sandwich was one of the modern sort, wearing a low-cut blouse and very tight trousers. Probably a university type doing a holiday job, I thought. She obviously didn't think much of me. I wasn't her sort. Not worth troubling about. Tall and well-built would have been more her sort. Like Eileen had said Hooky was. By now I felt more certain than ever that it was the man called Hooky who had come to the shop that day. And of course he would have got on famously with the low-cut blouse and the tight, bottom-hugging trousers.

I could afford to put up with her off-hand manner. I found it rather amusing. I wondered if she had read the papers when they were full of what happened at Wardle Gardens and what her reaction would be if she knew who I was.

When I came to pay the bill she actually thawed out a bit.

'Going far?' she asked.

'Round about.'

'There are some nice little places close by. Barwold for instance. Do you know that?'

I looked dumb. 'I don't know any of the places round here,' I told her. 'I'm a stranger in these parts.'

As I drove on I couldn't get the image of that girl and her tight trousers out of my mind. I had lewd thoughts about her. Lewd thoughts about her and the man Hooky. Lewd thoughts about Hooky and the other woman; the tall, laughing whore sitting at the bar of the Ram advising me to have the Pimms I hadn't dared to ask for in the pub I had just left. It doesn't trouble me having lewd thoughts about women; if the Lord didn't want me to have them he wouldn't put them into my head, would he?

When I got to Barwold I stopped the car a little way down the road from the lych gate and went into the church-yard.

Untidy and ill-kept Sergeant Wilson had called it. I suppose it was, but I liked it that way, it suited me. I didn't want it swept and garnished and smart and tarmacky. I liked the old untended drooping trees and the uncut grass that almost hid many of the headstones.

The grave I had come to look at, her grave, had got its own stone now. A pretentious affair which must have cost a lot and didn't say much – just her name and dates and a verse from some fatuous hymn, nothing about how she died; I thought they might at least have given that a mention.

'Tragic, wasn't it?'

The words startled me. In a curious way I had to come to think of Barwold churchyard as a sort of secret place, private to me. I felt at home there, and now suddenly there was someone else, a stranger, saying 'Tragic, wasn't it?'

Not quite a stranger, though. I might be a stranger to him but he wasn't one to me. I had seen him before. On the day of the funeral. His surplice flapping in the wind. His theatrical voice booming out about dust and ashes. Earning his fee.

'Tragic?' I said, as though I had no idea what he was talking about.

'She was murdered, you know. The Wardle Gardens murder in Dunsly. They never caught the man who did it, and I don't suppose they ever will.'

I wanted to say I sincerely hope not. I was rather enjoying this; but I kept my head. I thought I'd cheer him up a bit.

'Oh, I don't know,' I said, 'the police are pretty good on

the whole.'

'You didn't know her, then?' he asked.

'Good Lord, no. I don't know anybody here. I'm just motoring through and I stopped off to have a look round. Churches and churchyards interest me.'

'I'm afraid we have to keep the church shut. Vandals, you know. We live in lawless times.'

'We do indeed,' I agreed. 'It's awful.'

I left the car where it was in the little-used lane by the side of the church and went into the village on foot. I walked slowly. I wasn't in a hurry. For one thing, it was just being in the place that mattered; for another, I realised that I didn't know exactly what I wanted to do.

I wanted to see Hooky, certainly, to try to find out why he had come into the shop talking about Barwold, and the best way to do that would obviously be through casual conversation in the place where I could be pretty sure of finding him, the bar of the Ram; but it was now after closing time and the Ram would be shut.

It occurred to me that if we suddenly ran into one another in the village street he might be curious to know what I was doing in Barwold and whether I had any particular interest in the place. I even began to wonder if I had been altogether wise to come there.

Not that that doubt lasted for long. I was in Barwold because I had to come there; because I was under the spell of the place; to talk with Hooky if possible, certainly; but beyond that, behind that and any other imagined reason, because the idea of the woman haunted me.

I couldn't explain it even to myself. I hadn't lain with a woman for years, and yet now my thoughts were filled with fantasies of this laughing whore, naked and desirable. Yet all the time I remembered the woman of the Elect People and how I felt after that and I knew I should hate myself.

The place was as sleepy as usual; it was mid-afternoon and in mid-afternoon in Barwold everyone seems to disappear; whether they all have siestas or not I don't know, but there just isn't anyone about.

The Ram was shut, and although I had known that I would find this I took it as some sort of a sign; that means I won't be seeing Hooky, I told myself, so I may as well go back. This was just fooling myself, of course. I knew I was fooling myself. I knew all the time I wasn't going back – not yet. I left the Ram behind and walked through the village to where it straggled out into nothing, to where Otter Lodge stood.

I stood looking at it just as I had done the first time I had seen it on the day of Dolly Winter's funeral.

It all looked exactly the same; the same sign 'Barwold Antiques, High class Furniture, Pictures, Silver. Inspection invited'; the same, or at any rate very similar pieces of furniture outside in the small front garden.

I wondered if the door would open and if she would come out again as she had done that morning, damned near naked, laughing and shameless; calling me a Peeping Tom, telling me to sod off.

Nobody came out and everything seemed curiously still; there wasn't any sign of movement anywhere. Then I saw there was a piece of paper stuck in the door, some sort of notice presumably, and after a moment's hesitation I went forward to read it. It had only one word on it – *Closed*. Nothing about when they would be back or anything like that, just *Closed*.

I told myself what an immense relief it was. Now I didn't have to see the whore; now I didn't have to bother about her; it was like shedding a burden.

This is what I told myself, and I did my best to believe it. But of course I didn't believe it. Not right deep inside myself. Or at any rate if in one way it could be called a relief it was also a huge disappointment. Now there was no point in my being there; now I wondered what I had come to Barwold for in the first place; now I wondered why the Lord had put it in my head to come if I was going to find nothing, if there wasn't going to be anything for me to do....

111

I walked back to the side lane where I had left the car and started the journey back. There was nothing to hurry for, and I didn't intend to hurry; the prospect of Eileen's company and conversation didn't hold any attractions for me. I decided to go back the long way round, through the by-lanes, taking my time.

There was one length of road where the banks rose high on either side and trees from on top of the banks met overhead so that you were actually going into a green tunnel. It was suddenly dark and gloomy and in a way a bit eerie.

At the end of the green tunnel the lane turned sharply and there, just at the bend, there was a car drawn up on the verge and a woman standing by it.

As soon as she saw me coming she raised a hand to stop me. She obviously wanted something, help of some kind. Broken down in some way, I thought, or run out of petrol perhaps. At any rate whatever the reason she was obviously delighted to see me.

I didn't know whether I was delighted to see her or not. Suddenly my mind was in a whirl again and I felt a little sick. The woman standing by a broken-down car, confidently signalling to me for help, was the laughing whore from Otter Lodge.

CHAPTER TEN

All the standard procedures had been put into operation automatically. The police surgeon had officially pronounced the victim dead; the scene of the murder had been marked off with white tape and a constable was on duty guarding it; the official photographer had taken all the shots he wanted and measurements taken to prepare a plan; the body had been removed to the mortuary; the fingerprint people had done preliminary work on the bodywork of the car and the car itself had been towed away for a more detailed examination; the ground for a considerable distance round had been searched, and would continue to be searched, for any possible clues.

All this was routine stuff and, subject to one or two minor delays due to other calls on a depleted staff, had been put into operation smoothly and quickly.

The front room in Chalky White's police cottage had been taken over as the temporary operations centre and it was there that Inspector Marsh sat talking to Sergeant Williams:

'I said there'd be another strangling.' There was almost a note of satisfaction in the inspector's voice.

'You did,' Sergeant Williams was forced to agree.

'You think it's just coincidence?'

'I don't say coincidence exactly, but there are such things as copy-cat killings; something gets written up in the press and half a dozen lunatics think they might as well have a go at it!'

Marsh nodded. 'True enough,' he admitted. 'As my old

chief used to say, if you jump to conclusions too quickly you probably land up in a hell of a mess. Funny it should happen so close to Barwold where that other woman is buried.'

'Chalky's upset; he doesn't like murder on his pitch.'

'I don't like murder anywhere,' the Inspector said. 'When I started I couldn't wait to get on my first murder case, now I'm getting too old; I'll settle for a nice quiet case of shoplifting now. Well, I suppose we have got to start asking questions; we had better have another word with the man who reported it. Get him in, will you?'

A fair-haired young man with a look of apprehension on his slightly bucolic features came in and was invited to sit down.

'You are George Dawson, is that right?'

'That's right, sir; George Dawson, and I've never been mixed up in anything like this before.'

'Take it easy, Mr Dawson. In a case like this we have to ask questions from anybody who can possibly help in any way. There's nothing to it; nothing to be nervous about, it's just a matter of getting the facts straight. I understand you keep the Ram Hotel in Barwold, is that correct?'

'The Ram Inn, sir. We don't call it a hotel, although we do put people up occasionally; there's one gentleman staying at the moment as it happens. Me and my mother keep it together; we are joint tenants of the brewery.'

'Tell us again what happened this afternoon. You had been visiting some farm or other, I think you said.'

'Westgate Farm. Mr Nash's place. Every now and again I get a sack of corn from him for the poultry. Mother likes her eggs fresh and we've always kept a couple of dozen hens at the back. White Wyandottes generally.'

'So you were on your way back from Mr Nash at Westgate?'

'From Westgate Farm, yes, that's right. I'd got the sack of corn in the boot and was coming back by way of what they call the old Drove Road.'

'Is that your normal way?'

'From Westgate Farm, yes. It's pretty well the only way. It's all little lanes and out of the way places but I don't mind that.'

'And what happened?'

'The road makes a bend, a corner like, by what they call the New Coppice, and I saw this car standing there. Well, I thought, that's a bit funny because I knew the car by sight.'

'You recognised it?'

'Yes. It belongs to the woman who runs the antiques shop in the village. Otter Lodge. We see quite a bit of her in the Ram. To tell you the truth when I saw the car standing there and realised whose it was I thought she might have gone into New Coppice for a bit of fun with someone.'

'What made you think differently?'

'I was just going to drive on, thinking it was no business of mine, when I saw this foot sticking out, behind the car, so of course I thought hallo, there's something up and I stopped to have a look.'

'And you found the dead woman lying on the ground behind the car?'

'I did, and it shook me. I don't want to get mixed up in any of this, I thought; this is a job for the Law, so I got back in my car and drove straight to Chalky White, that's PC White of course.'

A series of questions followed about the exact position the body was lying in; about the time when the discovery was made; about whether anything had been handled or moved in any way. George Dawson's answers to all these points were straightforward enough but not particularly helpful and Inspector Marsh switched to another aspect of things.

'You say you saw a good deal of the dead woman in the Ram?'

'Yes. She was in most days one way or another.'

'Would you say she drank a lot?'

'A fair bit.'

115

'Did she come in alone or with anyone?'

'Not often alone. Usually she'd have a man with her.'

'What man?'

'Well, some people say he was her husband, some people say he wasn't; the man as runs the antique business with her.'

'Did they seem to be on good terms?'

'Mostly. I've heard them quarrel.'

'You have? What about?'

'I can't remember. I think they could both be pretty short tempered.'

'You mean that the man lost his temper with her?'

'I think she riled him at times.'

'Did she ever come in with any other man?'

'Well, there's this gentleman staying in the Ram. I'm bound to say she seemed pretty friendly with him too.'

'That's a man by the name of Hefferman, isn't it?'

'That's right. Mr Hefferman.'

'What do you know about him?'

'Well, nothing really. He's a very nice gentleman to deal with, very open handed.'

'Would you say he drinks a lot?'

'He's not a teetotaller.'

'What does he do all day?'

'I think he's up at Otter Lodge quite a lot.'

'Have you heard him quarrelling with the dead woman?'

'No. I'd say she was pretty fond of him.'

'Do you mean they were fond of one another?'

'I couldn't say anything about that.'

Three days later – three days which had been busy with a great deal of behind the scenes police activity, looking up records, searching old newspaper files, asking questions and generally gathering information – Inspector Marsh and his sergeant sat talking together again.

'I almost wish she hadn't been strangled,' Marsh said unexpectedly after some minutes of silent thought.

The remark surprised Sergeant Wilson. 'I thought you

were pleased to have your theory vindicated,' he said.

'I'm beginning to think your theory of a copy-cat killing is more likely to be right,' Marsh said. 'It seems very unlikely that Hadleigh was tied up in any way with the Wardle Gardens job.'

'And you think he's tied up with this one?'

'I think it's only common sense to take a look at the things under one's nose, not to miss the obvious things; they may not turn out to be the right ones in the end but at least we ought to look at them. So what have we got here? The old classic situation. Adam and Eve and Punchme. A woman's two men. The woman was a high-flyer. We know something about her now. Good family, her father a regular officer and so on. But of course that meant nothing to her. She's one of the modern sort. According to Chalky White half the time at the Otter Lodge place she'd be going about with more clothes off than on. She and the Hadleigh man weren't married, of course, and never likely to be either.'

'Anything known about him?'

'He hasn't got any form; but he seems to have been a proper young b.f. Came in for a lot of money, thirty thousand or so, a couple of years back and practically threw it out of the window. The good old formula, wine, women and song, though I doubt if he did much actual singing. A pigeon for the plucking if ever there was one and from all accounts she was a pretty good plucker. Then this chap Hefferman comes on the scene—'

'Why? Sergeant Wilson interrupted. 'That's something that puzzles me; why should Hefferman come to stay at the Ram in Barwold? Love of the countryside? Just a holiday? But he isn't your ordinary tourist sort surely? Was he pally with the dead woman before he came here? An old flame?'

'Could have been. Could well have been. We don't know, yet. There's a lot about Mr Hefferman we don't know yet. But we soon will, they're finding out for us up in the smoke. What we do know is that he did, in fact, come to Barwold and according to all accounts became pretty close friends with the couple at Otter Lodge.'

'With one of them at any rate.'

'You've had a word with Mrs Dawson?'

'I've talked to her a couple of times.'

'What sort is she?'

'Straightforward, decent, motherly type. Full of common sense, I'd say. Incidentally, it's no good going to her for a bad report on Hefferman; he's put the come-hither on her; she likes him, reckons he's a proper gentleman. Of course this business has upset her because the Fellingham girl used to come into the Ram a lot.'

'With Hadleigh.'

'Sometimes; sometimes not.'

'Did she ever hear them quarrelling?'

'She says they had words occasionally and once she did hear Hadleigh saying something to Hefferman about having had a blazing row.'

Inspector Marsh considered for a minute in silence, drumming with his fingers on the table (a habit which Sergeant Wilson found peculiarly irritating); at last he said, 'Well, it doesn't amount to much at present, but it may develop. You never know. Great oaks from little acorns. I'm anxious to hear more about Hefferman, I must say; Mrs Dawson may reckon he's a perfect gentleman, I'm not so sure. Meanwhile I'm going up to Otter Lodge to have another session with Hadleigh.'

Otter Lodge had been shut ever since Tessa's death and the *Closed* notice hung permanently on the door. Lynton Hadleigh had scarcely moved out of the place. He was frightened by the mere idea of death, and being brought into close and brutal contact with it had shaken him badly. He would dearly have liked to go down to the Ram, but he shrank from the thought of the publicity involved – furtive glances, whisperings, people looking at him and then quickly away again, saying things to one another in undertones. So instead of drinking at the Ram under Mrs Dawson's watchful eye he sat in Otter Lodge drinking alone, and drinking too much.

When he went to the door and saw who his visitor was his heart sank. He had already answered a lot of questions and he didn't want to have any more to do with the police. The old idea of what a lark it would be to nick a bobby's helmet had no connection at all, he had discovered, with the sort of questioning Inspector Marsh had subjected him to. The police inspector had been polite – just – but hostile, and Hadleigh was scared of him.

'Did you want to see me, Inspector?' he asked, rather superfluously.

'If you can spare a minute or two, Mr Hadleigh.'

'I suppose you had better come in then.'

Marsh was already in; he had long since learnt the value of getting a foot in the door and following up that first foot with another one as soon as possible.

'I expect you'd like to join me in a drink,' Hadleigh suggested.

'Not on duty, thank you.'

'Oh well – perhaps you'll excuse me.'

Marsh watched whilst a generous whisky – very obviously not the first one of the day – was poured out and a minimum of soda squirted into it. Hadleigh took a sip from the newly charged glass and gained some Dutch courage from it.

'I've already told you all I can, you know,' he said. 'I really can't see—'

'That's all right, Mr Hadleigh. I'm sure you think you've told us all you can. But lots of people tell us lots of things; it's a question of sorting everything out. And people forget things, you know. You may have forgotten something.'

'I don't think I have.'

'You knew Miss Fellingham before coming to Barwold, is that right?'

'Yes, I've told you about that. My uncle left me a lot of furniture and we decided to start up in the antique business with it.'

119

'And the two of you were intimate friends?'

'You can put it that way if you like; yes, we were intimate friends.'

'But you never married?'

'That's not a crime, is it?'

'Murder's a crime, Mr Hadleigh, that's what we are trying to find out about. You and Miss Fellingham always got on well together, did you?'

'I've just told you, we were intimate friends.'

'You never quarrelled?'

'I didn't say we never quarrelled, I said we were good friends.'

The inspector paused for a moment to consult his notes and Hadleigh took a generous sip of his drink and devoutly hoped there wasn't much questioning to come.

Putting his notebook away for the moment Marsh continued, 'At about three-forty in the afternoon of the day Miss Fellingham was murdered Police Constable White was passing the open gateway of the yard of the Ram Inn and he stated that he saw you there talking to a man called Hefferman who was apparently cleaning his car – do you remember that, Mr Hadleigh?'

Hadleigh nodded.

Marsh consulted his notebook again. 'And PC White says he overheard you say, 'That's what finally made me see red' or words very much to that effect; do you remember that also?'

'I – I can't remember now what we said to one another, exactly. I think we were talking about dog licences.'

'Dog licences?'

'About some people objecting to paying thirty-seven and a half pence for a licence.'

'And you said that made you see red?'

'I may have done; ask Mr Hefferman, I'm sure he'll remember we were talking about licences.'

Marsh's smile was bleak. 'Possibly,' he said. 'Would you

care to tell me once again about your movements on that day?'

Several successive sips emboldened Hadleigh to reply, 'I've told you all about that once, why should I go over it all again?'

'Well, Mr Hadleigh, we sometimes get things wrong and I want to be sure that I get this right; now then, according to my notes here, you and Miss Fellingham had some sort of disagreement in the morning, is that so?'

'Yes we did; you've got it in your notes already.'

'Did you quarrel violently?'

'We had a disagreement.'

'And you don't want to tell me what it was about?'

'Why should I?'

The Inspector made no comment on this and he went on, 'And what did you do then?'

'I went out of the house and walked about.'

'Just walked about?'

'Yes. I was upset.'

'So the quarrel was fairly violent, I take it.'

'I wanted to be away from the house for a while and out in the fresh air, so I went for a walk.'

'Did you see anybody on this walk?'

'I didn't speak with anyone; I didn't feel like speaking to anyone.'

'I should have thought that in circumstances such as those it would have been natural for a gentleman like yourself to go down to the local, the Ram, and have a drink.'

'I didn't want to go to the Ram.'

'Why not, Mr Hadleigh? Was there somebody there you didn't want to meet?'

'I didn't say that. I just didn't want to go to the Ram. It's not a crime not to have a drink, is it?'

'So you walked about and finally ended up outside the Ram yard talking with the man Hefferman who was

121

washing his car.'

'He wasn't washing it, dusting it more.'

'Then you went back to Otter Lodge. Miss Fellingham wasn't there and some time later you heard of her death, and that was the first you knew about it – I've got that right, haven't I?'

'As you've got it all written down you won't have to ask me any more questions about it, will you?'

Inspector Marsh put his notebook away. He made no promises.

'Thank you Mr Hadleigh,' he said, 'that's all – for the present.'

Back in his temporary office the inspector began to tidy up the papers on his desk, hoping for the unusual bonus of an early getaway and feeling that he was finished with interviewing for the day.

Matters turned out slightly differently.

Sergeant Wilson put his head round the door to announce, 'That chap from the Ram wants a word with you, boss.'

'George Dawson?'

'No; the one staying there, Hefferman.'

'Hefferman? What does he want?'

Sergeant Wilson grinned. 'He says he wants to whisper words of warning and wisdom into your shell-like ear, sir,' he replied.

The inspector's ears were far from shell-like, they were unusually large and outstanding; hence the sergeant's grin.

Marsh sat down again at the desk he had been on the point of leaving. 'Show him in,' he said.

Hooky settled his large frame on the somewhat inadequate chair available and grinned amiably at the Inspector, and, it would seem, at the world at large.

'You are Inspector Vivian Marsh of the Dunsly CID, I believe,' he led off, 'is that right?'

'I am.'

'Now, I don't want to upset you, Inspector, so don't get

122

alarmed; there's nothing to worry about, just a few simple questions; that's what you tell the poor so-and-sos when you're grilling them, isn't it? Then you proceed to put them through it. Quite right, too. I'm all for the Law having a heavy hand; there are too many villains about. That's why I don't want to see you making a bit of a b.f. of yourself, old sport.'

Marsh sighed; he had had a full day; he wanted to get back to Mrs Marsh and an armchair in front of the box; he didn't want to have to cope with cheerful exuberance no doubt originally engendered in the Ram; on the other hand he did want to have a good look at the happy extrovert sitting opposite him.

'Does all this mean that you've got some information to give me, Mr Hefferman?' he asked coldly.

'Don't get peeved, old sport, don't get peeved. Information, yes; and advice too. All for nix. Free.'

'I wasn't proposing to pay you anything.'

'I'm sure you weren't. A pretty mean lot, the Law, when it's a matter of cash. Which makes my conduct all the more, if I could pronounce the next word I'd use it, mag— something.'

'Magnanimous perhaps?'

'You're a brainy bird, Inspector, a clever fellow; but not quite clever enough over your current problem.'

'I'm always willing to learn.'

'That's what the girl told the soldier; and she learnt quite a lot. I hear that enquiries have been made about me, on your behalf, at my modest headquarters in London.'

'We make enquiries about a lot of people.'

'I'm sure you do. You're a nosey lot. But you can give up hunting this particular hare. You're wasting your time; which of course means my time; I'm a taxpayer, I pay your wages don't forget. Scotland Yard already knows a good deal about me.'

'That doesn't surprise me in the least.'

'And I know a number of men at the Yard.'

'How so, Mr Hefferman?'

'What do you dislike most in the world, Inspector?'

'Characters who come in here at the end of a long day, half cut, and proceed to explain how wonderful they themselves are and what fools all policemen are. I find them very boring.'

Hooky gave a burst of uninhibited laughter. 'Touché!' he cried. 'A hit, a palpable hit. One up to the Law. I'm prepared to bet a considerable sum, Inspector Marsh, that one of the things you dislike most is what I am sure you would call a Private Eye.'

'You're perfectly right. Can't stand 'em. No use for 'em. Frauds most of 'em.'

'Harsh words, my friend, harsh words. And probably actionable. I'm a Private Investigator myself.'

'You are?'

'Well established in Regency House, Gerrard Mews, in the not particularly salubrious region of Soho. The trusted friend and adviser of anyone who cares to employ me.'

'And presumably such fools exist,' Marsh said. 'What are you doing in Barwold?'

'You wouldn't want me to betray a professional confidence, surely?'

'Does that mean you are here on some sort of a job?'

'It means I am minding my own business, Inspector.'

Marsh nodded and rose to indicate that as far as he was concerned the interview was at an end.

'Well, just be sure that you stick to your own business,' he said. 'I don't want any so-called private investigator messing about in mine, and don't be surprised if I have a number of questions to ask you about this Otter Lodge affair. For the moment, I suppose, you'll be going back to the bar of the Ram?'

'Like a homing pigeon,' Hooky assured him happily.

CHAPTER ELEVEN

Hove

My dear nephew,

I have been in bed for most of the week with an old fashioned cold which the doctor insists on calling influenza. This afternoon, unable to stand the ministrations of my daily woman any longer, I got up, rather shakily I must admit, and began to pick up the threads again.

Looking through *The Times*, which I hadn't bothered to read for three or four days, I was horrified to read the news about Tessa Fellingham.

I have written to her father, of course – though what good is a letter in such circumstances and what can you put in it, anyway?

When I suggested to you that the girl might be getting herself involved with bad company I had no idea that things would turn out like this.

You have a genius, of course, for getting mixed up in unsavoury matters. I devoutly hope that you have had nothing to do with this dreadful affair. Poor Harry F. will be badly upset. I think you should go and see him. When you do, tell him that as soon as I feel well enough to travel I will come up to London and call on him myself – oh, Hooky, I am an old woman now and in my time this world of ours has degenerated from a decent place, fit to live in, to a noisy nightmare. I would say it has gone to the dogs except that all the dogs I have known in my life have been so much nicer than most humans; you don't have a dog, I believe, your morals might improve if you had.

Your affectionate aunt
Theresa Page-Foley

P.S. Has the man T. was living with been arrested yet?

Hooky read his aunt's letter a couple of times and was touched by it. *I'm an old woman now* was a confession which he hadn't often heard from Theresa Page-Foley, that straight-backed upholder of standards, that indomitable scorner of weaknesses.

I think you should go and see him – Hooky realised that, as usual, the old lady from Hove had hit the nail on the head; but a visit to Tessa Fellingham's father was not something he looked forward to with any pleasure. He found it difficult to imagine the sort of conversation you could use when talking with a man whose daughter had recently been strangled.

Telling Mrs Dawson to keep his room for him and assuring her that he would be back in a few days, Hooky climbed into his Jag and motored in leisurely fashion to the Great Wen. On his way he pondered again on his aunt's letter, concentrating finally on the postscript which, on reflection, struck him as being the most important sentence in the whole thing.

Lynton Hadleigh had not yet been arrested, but it was pretty obvious that the world, reading titillating accounts of the affair in the daily press, expected that he soon would be; and, as Hooky knew only too well, if the police had an obvious suspect in their sights the poor devil was apt to have a mighty thin time of it.

What sort of case could be built up against Hadleigh

Hooky didn't know; what he did know was that with a murder case on their hands the police would go to almost any length to get somebody in the dock for it; and that, despite all bland assertions about being innocent till proved guilty, once a man is in the dock he is more than half way to jail.

It was possible, Hooky had to acknowledge, turning the matter over in that part of his mind not occupied with avoiding the hazards of the M4, that Lynton Hadleigh deserved to be in the dock; deserved to go to jail; that he was guilty. It was certain that he would fare badly under examination by a bullying counsel for the prosecution; even more certain that twelve good men and true, agreeably conscious of their own moral superiority, would be likely to take a poor view of him.

On balance Hooky didn't think Hadleigh was a murderer; what he was quite certain of, however, was that under the sort of prolonged and intensive questioning to which he would be subjected he was only too likely to say a lot of silly things, things which could be made to sound a great deal worse than silly when repeated in court.

In Regency House Roly Watkins was as refreshingly sardonic as ever.

'Nice little lot you've been mixing with,' was his greeting. 'I told you not to go into those foreign parts, didn't I? Much better to have stayed at home and got into trouble here. The Law has been round asking questions about you like nobody's business.'

This didn't surprise Hooky, who had expected Inspector Marsh to set routine enquiries in train.

'I hope you gave a good account of me,' he told Roly with a grin.

'I said as you were the most hard-working, moral, sober, law-abiding citizen in the whole of London,' Roly assured him, 'and may Heaven forgive me for such a pack of lies. Who did it?'

'How should I know?'

'I suppose it was that chap as ran the antiques shop with her.'

'Why should you think that?'

'Because I wasn't born yesterday; I can read between the lines as well as anybody else.'

'I'm astonished to hear that you can read at all,' Hooky said crossly.

Hooky approached the flat in Castle Square with reluctance, dislike of the forthcoming interview slowing down his usual brisk pace to something much more sedate. He rang the bell and after a lengthy pause the door was opened by Henry Fellingham himself. Hooky was shocked to see how the little man's square-shouldered, military bearing had deserted him; he looked shrunken and diminished; 'crumpled' was Hooky's initial summing-up. In the severely tidy living room Hooky was offered, and gladly accepted, a large Scotch and soda; Fellingham contented himself with a glass of Madeira.

'Used to be able to get it anywhere in London at one time,' he said, 'not so easy nowadays. I came to like it as a young man and I've stuck to it ever since, which shows either steadfastness or a lack of initiative, according to how you look at things; but you haven't come here to talk about my taste in wine – are you able to tell me anything more about the business at Barwold?'

'Nothing substantial; no, I'm afraid I can't.'

Fellingham nodded. He might have been relieved. It was difficult to tell.

'My aunt suggested I should come to see you.'

'Ah, Theresa.' The little man seemed glad to have a non-Barwold subject to talk about. 'How is she? She must be getting on now of course – which of us isn't? – but I don't suppose she has made many concessions to age; as I recall it she never made many concessions to anything; or to anybody for that matter. I remember once—'

Hooky, who like many men who are physically brave was something of a moral coward, was only too glad to listen whilst his host rambled on in reminiscences which, if they weren't particularly interesting in themselves, at least had the merit of having nothing to do with Barwold.

Suddenly, with an abrupt change of tone, and virtually in the middle of an unfinished anecdote, Fellingham said, 'We've got to talk about it, so we may as well do so – if there's anything to say. It's worse for Nancy than for me, of course. She's upstairs in bed. She'll never get up again now. I had to tell her; she'd have seen about it in the papers. You'd think dying of cancer would be enough, wouldn't you, without having this as well.'

Fatuous expressions of sympathy threatened to rise to Hooky's lips. Wisely he suppressed them. He said nothing. There was nothing to say.

'The funny thing is,' Fellingham went on, 'that I don't feel any particular personal animosity against that man Hadleigh. Perhaps I ought to be blazingly angry with him. But I'm not. If I saw him here this minute I wouldn't want to strike him. If he gets sent to jail for ten years or so I shan't take any pleasure in it. I suppose he will go to jail, won't he?'

'If he's guilty.'

Fellingham nodded and said, almost to himself, 'I suppose I failed somewhere along the line in bringing the girl up; maybe we are all guilty in a way.'

Hooky, who very seldom refused a second drink, did so now and was mightily relieved to find himself outside in Castle Square once more. Whether Hove would consider his account of the interview satisfactory he very much doubted; satisfying the exacting standards of Hove was a difficult matter, thunderbolts from Hove were as inevitable and inescapable as those from Jove and had equally to be endured.

He didn't feel inclined to face the chirpy inquisitiveness of Roly Watkins again, so as soon as he was reunited with the Jag he turned her radiator in a nor'westerly direction and steered for the Cotswold hills.

In the Ram he found a very different Mrs Dawson from the usual placid person he knew. Martha Dawson was upset and she told him so volubly as soon as she saw him.

He was touched by her evident pleasure at his return. 'Mr Hefferman,' she told him, 'I'm glad to see you back, I really am. You're somebody I can talk to. And there aren't many of them. Most of them don't listen and don't know anything anyway.'

'What's the trouble, Mrs D?'

'Nothing has been the same in the Ram since that poor girl got herself murdered. People say it must have been her own fault, well I don't know about that. I don't say as she was a saint, which of us is?' (Which, indeed, Hooky thought, remembering once again that awkward sentence *maybe we are all guilty in a way*.) 'But this has upset everybody,' Mrs Dawson went on. 'Mr Hadleigh never comes in now and you would think he would want a drink. I expect he's afraid of the newspaper men. They've been swarming in the place, trying to get anything they can out of everybody. Vultures I call them.'

'That's nothing to what I could call them Mrs D,' Hooky assured her cheerfully, 'but I wouldn't like to offend your innocent ears. Has the Fleet Street pack been baying after you?'

'It's poor George they've been at most, because he was the one who – well, you know what I mean, he found it didn't he? Found the body. And even if you are a very good son, which George always has been to me, it doesn't necessarily follow that you are particularly bright, does it? And the police keep coming to see him too. He's already told them all he can, but they never seem satisfied and they keep on with their questions. Which reminds me, Mr Hefferman, that Inspector Marsh has left a message for you – as soon as you're back would you go and have a word with him at Chalky White's cottage. I told him it wasn't up to me to make your arrangements for you, but when I saw you I'd pass his message on – *if* I remembered, I told him, I didn't promise anything.'

'Good for you, Mrs D,' Hooky laughed. 'I'll have to have you as my private secretary yet.'

'If I was twenty years younger you wouldn't have to ask me twice I can tell you,' Martha Dawson avowed.

In the small living room of Chalky White's cottage Hooky asked cheerfully, 'You wanted to see me about something?'

'Only if you are sober,' Marsh told him. 'Last time you came here you weren't.' The inspector had had a day filled with niggling details and none of his enquiries seemed to be getting anywhere. He wasn't in the best of moods.

'Inspector,' Hooky assured him earnestly, 'you see before you a man in the sad state of extreme sobriety. I am as sober as a judge; more sober than some judges I have known. If at this moment you produced a bottle of good malt whisky my opinion of the force would rise dramatically.'

'I'm a police officer,' Marsh answered, 'not a publican. And as an experienced officer let me tell you that I think it's very silly of you, Hefferman, to put it mildly, not to tell me exactly what you are doing here in Barwold.'

'Why should I pander to the inquisitiveness of the police?'

'That's exactly the sort of silly attitude I'm warning you against. A crime has been committed here in Barwold. A woman has been murdered. It is, therefore, the obvious duty of the police to find out what a stranger to the place was doing here, especially one who was apparently on friendly terms with the murdered woman and with her associate.'

'It's the associate you're after, isn't it?'

'We're after whoever killed Tessa Fellingham.'

'I hope you find him – or her.'

'Her?'

'Anyone can commit a murder, that's one of your standard maxims surely.'

The inspector turned to some notes on his desk and after perusal of them looked up again and said, 'It seems that you are acquainted with Lieutenant Colonel Fellingham, the murdered girl's father?'

Hooky grinned and said, 'Well done, I like to see you boys doing your homework. Yes, I know the Colonel.'

'You wouldn't care to elaborate on that a bit?'

Hooky pondered for a few moments before coming to a decision. Why shouldn't he, as the inspector put it, elaborate? It could do no harm and it might save trouble in the end.'

'Have you got an aunt, Inspector?' he enquired.

Marsh looked up in surprise. 'An aunt? Yes, I've got an aunt. What's that to do with anything?'

'It depends on the quality of the aunt. Where does yours live?'

'In Basingstoke.'

Hooky shook his head. 'Not in the same league,' he said. 'My aunt rules the roost in Hove and she ranks high in the She-Who-Must-Be-Obeyed stakes. She and Colonel Fellingham were buddies in the old days. Difficult to imagine anyone being a really close buddy of Aunt Theresa but those were heroic times.

'When Fellingham married, the daughter, Tessa, grew up a misfit. She couldn't get on with her father and mother and they didn't know how to communicate with her. Don't ask me whose fault it was. I don't know. Probably nobody's; possibly everybody's; we're all guilty in a way, wouldn't you say? Anyway the girl went off on her own ploys, hopping in and out of quite a few beds I wouldn't wonder.

'There wasn't much her father could do about it, but naturally he was worried, especially as his wife is dying of cancer. He got more worried than ever when Tessa took up with Lynton Hadleigh, who had made something of a reputation for himself by coming in for thirty thousand quid and throwing it around. My Aunt Theresa was the

132

girl's godmother so, wanting to get advice from somebody, Fellingham went to her; and do you know what that wise woman said, Inspector?'

'Tell me.'

'She said he couldn't do better than engage the services of the most efficient, most discreet, most satisfactory private investigator in London, so of course I got the job.'

'Leaving out the self-advertising bits, what job exactly?'

'Finding out all I could about Lynton Hadleigh, and whether Tessa had got herself tied up with a real crook or not.'

'And had she?'

Hooky shook his head. 'In my opinion Hadleigh isn't a crook,' he said. 'He may be silly, I think he *is* silly; he may be weak, I think he *is* weak; but he's no real criminal.'

'Weak and silly characters can commit murders.'

The two men looked long and hard at one another and finally Hooky broke silence.

'Like I said, you're after him, aren't you?'

'Like I told you, we are after whoever killed Tessa Fellingham. I don't know how much you found out about Hadleigh – did you discover, for instance, that four years ago he was mixed up in assaulting the doorkeeper of a night club in Chelsea?'

Hooky, to whom this disturbing item of news came as a surprise, replied stuffily that he wasn't prepared to discuss with anyone how far he had got in a particular case; a reply which made Inspector Marsh laugh heartily. 'Quite right,' he approved. 'When you don't know anything, don't say anything. I don't like private investigators, Hefferman; in fact I hate the whole tribe of them. I don't say that I hate you personally, so I'll give you a piece of advice – stop meddling in things that belong to the professionals; pack up and go; get out of my hair before I get annoyed.'

Hooky walked away from Chalky White's cottage in thoughtful mood. The interview with Inspector Marsh had disturbed him. He kept telling himself that there was no

133

real cause for alarm, the police might be suspicious about Lynton Hadleigh but being suspicious was a long way from having any sort of proof; yet this platitude didn't really carry much weight. Proof? Actual hard, direct, indisputable proof? Hooky knew only too well that in the vast majority of murder cases such proof, by the very nature of things, didn't exist. Men were convicted and found guilty on circumstantial evidence cleverly manipulated by skilful counsel whose concern was not to see justice done but to secure a verdict.

On his way to Otter Lodge, whither he was bound, he deliberately made a detour through the churchyard. It was as untidy and as unkempt as ever, the long uncut grass straggling all over the place, the unswept leaves lying everywhere. Except for Hooky himself the place was deserted. He paused for a moment by the place where Dolly Winter was buried and wondered whether the little newsagent from Dunsly had been back to stand by the grave and stare down at it.

At Otter Lodge the *Closed* notice was again in evidence, but persistent knockings and ringings eventually brought Hadleigh to the door. He professed himself delighted to see Hooky. 'I've been feeling as lonely as hell,' he declared, and it was obvious that he had been taking palliatives against such lonely feelings.

'It's persecution,' he told Hooky, talking loudly and rapidly, 'that's what it is, persecution. I daren't go out. If I do everybody stares at me; people I pass in the street naturally turn round to look at me. I know what they are all thinking. They don't have to tell me. They're thinking – *there's the man who did it*. And it's all the fault of the police. It's the fault of that horrible inspector man and his equally horrible sergeant. They never stop asking me questions—'

'Take it easy,' Hooky broke in, 'have a breather. There's plenty of time to talk things over. What's in that bottle?'

'Glenfiddich, thank heavens I've got a stock in.'

'A wise provision,' Hooky agreed. 'Pour out a very large

one for me and a very small one for yourself; at a guess you've done pretty well already. What sort of questions has Marsh been asking?'

Hadleigh poured out two drinks equally generous in size and handed one to Hooky. 'Always the same questions,' he answered. 'What was I doing on the day Tessa was killed.'

'And what were you doing?'

'I went for a walk. Tessa and I had an up-and-downer and I took myself off for a walk. I just couldn't stand being in the house with her any more so I went outside to be by myself a while.'

'Where did you go to?'

'Round about. God damn it, Hooky, I don't know what names the natives give to the miserable muddy lanes round here and I'll bet you don't either. I walked about.'

'Did you see anybody?'

'I didn't speak to anybody, if that's what you mean. I might have seen someone. I forget. You're as bad as the Inspector. Can't you drink your Scotch and stop asking these damned questions.'

Excellent advice, Hooky thought. He followed it and fell to considering. '*I walked about, just walked about*—'; difficult for the prosecution to prove it actually untrue, but not at all difficult to make it sound a feeble sort of defence.

'What's all this about beating up the bouncer in a Chelsea night spot?' he asked.

Hadleigh stared at him in indignant astonishment. 'That was four years ago,' he cried. 'How on earth did you get hold of that story?'

'I didn't get hold of it. Marsh did.'

'My God, is there anything they don't pry into?'

'Not much. Not when they're after someone. What happened?'

'Nothing happened. Nothing much anyway. We were quite a party and nobody had signed the pledge. This chap on the door got a bit fresh and said something to one of the girls. I told him to mind his manners and there was a bit of a punch-up. That's all. What's it got to do with this business of Tessa?'

Hooky sighed. Babes and sucklings, he thought. '. . .*and so ladies and gentlemen of the jury we have here clear evidence of a man liable to sudden outbursts of temper and violence. A man who has actually been guilty of such an outburst in the past. . .*' he could hear prosecuting counsel's words even if Hadleigh couldn't.

'What did you quarrel with Tessa about?' he asked.

'I told you in the Ram one evening.'

'No, you didn't. Not properly. You started to tell me but the pure stream of narrative became muddied by tributaries from the bar, vodka lime and soda if I remember correctly.'

'Well, this evening it's Glenfiddich – where's your glass?'

Hooky laid a restraining hand on the bottle. 'Not yet, old sport,' he said. 'Plenty of time yet. Sing me the songs of yesteryear, tell me again what you started to say about Tessa that evening in the Ram. Something about going too far, wasn't it?'

'It *was* going too far and I told her so at the time. Mind you, Hooky, it took a bit of nerve to stand up to Tessa and tell her anything, especially when she had her shooting boots on; but over this thing about the old girl's china I did it. I stood up to Tessa and told her straight it was over the odds.'

'Brave fellow. The old girl's china – what was that?'

'Tessa got lost one day motoring round in the wilds. She never had much bump of locality. She got lost and stopped to ask the way. In any cottage or farm house she always kept an eye open for possible bargains in the way of furniture or pictures and so on; in the antique business you always do, it's automatic. There was some sort of domestic rumpus, involving a cat and a parrot, which Tessa sorted out and in the course of it she spied some china. Four pieces which she knew were Chelsea and which looked really good. Unfortunately the old girl had already sworn blind that nothing would ever persuade her to sell a single thing;

136

so what's the good of telling me all this I asked Tessa and she told me not to be so thick; as buying the china figures was out of the question we were going to steal them, she and I together.'

'And did you?'

'No. I refused.'

Hooky gave a sigh of relief. 'Thank the Lord for that,' he said. 'That's one complication we can do without. If Marsh could pin a charge of theft on you he would be only too delighted. When you're stoning a man every pebble helps.'

'I didn't steal the Chelsea figures; but Tessa did.'

'*She did?*'

'Don't you remember that business of a woman in an out-of-the way place being pushed into the living room and locked in?'

'Yes; but I had no idea it was Tessa who did it.'

'Well, it was. She stole the Chelsea figures and that's what we had our final row about.'

'And where are the china figures now?'

'Here. In this house. In the wardrobe in the bedroom upstairs, to be precise.'

Hooky's hand was no longer a restraining one; now it was he who reached for the comforting bottle to replenish their two glasses. 'My God, Hadleigh, old sport,' he said, 'you've a genius for getting yourself into trouble.'

CHAPTER TWELVE

The odd thing is that although I make most of my living from selling newspapers I hardly ever read the things. Aunt Mamie, who brought me up, wouldn't have a newspaper in the house; the only periodical she read was a magazine called *Flame* which circulated among the Elect People; she reckoned that the whole daily press was wicked. Eileen, of course, can't keep her nose out of the papers; as far as she's concerned if she sees a thing in print it's gospel. I don't know how she gets on when she reads two completely different accounts in two different papers of the same thing; I suppose the answer is that she doesn't really take in what she reads.

How much she took in of the murder cases she read about I don't know, but if a murder was reported in the papers she read all about it. Every word. Especially, of course, any local affair like the one in Wardle Gardens and the woman in Barwold.

'Funny that one of them should be buried in Barwold and the other be killed there,' she said, and she gave me that sly look which I knew meant that she had something up her sleeve. I wasn't afraid of her in any way; not yet; but I thought I might have to be careful. She was stupid, of course; but stupid people can be dangerous.

'What's funny about it?' I asked.

'Well, it *is* funny, that's all, both of them being connected with Barwold.'

'Coincidence,' I told her. 'Everyone has to live some-where.'

I had been out most of the morning and I was just about to ask if anything had happened whilst I was away when she forestalled me.

'The man from the gymnasium came in,' she said, and I understood what that sly look of hers was about.

Terry O'Donovan had never been to the shop before; he got his papers and cigarettes and anything else he wanted in that line from a shop just round the corner from the gym.

'Terry O'Donovan?'

'If that's his name; from O'Donovan's gymnasium he said he was.'

'What did he want?'

'He was asking why you haven't been going there lately.'

I gave up going to O'Donovan's gymnasium after I killed the whore in Wardle Gardens. I can't explain exactly why I gave up. I suppose I felt in an obscure way that the less I appeared in public in any shape or form the better. Anyway, I did give up going; but I didn't tell Eileen I had given up. I went out of the house on Tuesday and Friday evenings as usual, but instead of going to O'Donovan's I walked about the streets, thinking.

'*Haven't* you been going there?' Eileen asked.

'I may have missed once or twice.'

'He said you hadn't been for weeks past.'

She was beginning to make me angry. 'Don't go on about it,' I told her, 'the Lord tells me where to go and what to do.'

A customer came in at that moment and nothing more was said about Tuesday and Friday evenings. I wasn't going to continue the subject and I suppose Eileen was afraid to; but I realised that she might be troublesome, dangerous even, and that I would have to watch her. I might have to take steps.

Inspector Marsh had been called to Dunsly to deal with something which over the telephone had been described as 'urgent business'. When he got to headquarters he discovered that the business was no more urgent than making arrangements for a forthcoming visit by the chief constable of the county. Not that the inspector regarded this as a trivial matter; Chief Constables were important people and proper arrangements had to be made to greet them – a little extra spit and polish, a little more care to make sure that awkward matters were swept safely under the carpet. These necessary affairs being attended to Marsh was glad to come back to Chalky White's cottage.

'Anything new?' he asked Sergeant Wilson.

'Nothing of any consequence. But a bit of an oddity. You remember that business at Pools?'

'Pools?'

'The out-of-the-way place where the old girl got locked in her own living room and some bits of china were taken.'

Marsh nodded.

'Well, the china has turned up again. All four pieces. At the end of her drive. She found them there this morning.'

'Any leads? She didn't see or hear anything?'

'Not a thing. She wouldn't be likely to. She's a bit deaf and she locks herself in pretty securely at night.'

'The pieces of china are all right? Not damaged in any way?'

'Apparently not.'

The inspector laughed. 'I wish all our problems would solve themselves as easily,' he said. 'There's plenty to worry about. Where's White?'

'Gone over Denstone way. Some young lads have got a grudge against a farmer there, or so he says, and have been letting his stock out at night. Just the sort of job Chalky likes, I reckon he'd make a good farmer's boy.'

The potentially good farmer's boy had an agreeable time at Denstone Farm. The farmer was reasonable; his wife plump and friendly; his home brewed cider eminently quaffable, so that it was midday before Chalky was back at base.

'Been riding the range?' Sergeant Wilson greeted him.

140

'Rounded all the stock up?'

'More or less.' Chalky smiled in an amiable way; he could afford to let the sergeant have his bit of fun, he was a pint and a half of good Cotswold cider better off than the sergeant.

'Those bits of china of yours have turned up.'

'What china is that, then?'

'The four pieces taken from the place at Pools. The old lady found them at the end of her drive this morning. You weren't anywhere near there during the night, I suppose?'

'I went by there yesterday evening, lateish.'

'See anything or anybody?'

'I wasn't looking in particular. Just cycling home. That chap from the Ram came by in that Jaguar of his, otherwise I didn't see anyone.'

Inspector Marsh had come into the room just in time to hear the last remark.

'*Who* did you say was there?' he asked sharply.

'That chap staying at the Ram, the one with the vintage car.'

'What was he doing there?'

Chalky looked blank. 'Doing, sir? I don't know. Nothing as far as I could see. He just came by in that Jag of his.'

'How far was he from Pools Cottage?'

'Pretty close. A quarter of a mile from the end of the drive, maybe.'

'What time was this?'

Chalky thought for a moment and then said, 'Round about nine, must have been. It was dark anyway.'

As soon as the inspector and his sergeant were alone again Marsh said, 'The old girl will have handled those bits of china pretty thoroughly I expect, so it's not much use trying for finger prints, I'm afraid.'

'You're not thinking that Hefferman had anything to do with lifting the china, are you sir?'

'I'm thinking that Hefferman is a bloody nuisance. I'm thinking that somehow or other he's mixed up in things

141

here more than we know about yet. I'm thinking that I'd like to have another word with him. Tell him, would you?'

Later, when Hooky was eventually rounded up in the Ram and then ushered into the inspector's presence, he decided to open the bowling with a brisk over.

'I suppose you realise that I'm losing valuable drinking time by coming here,' he led off.

Marsh smiled in deceptively friendly fashion. 'I thought of that,' he replied, producing a bottle from under his desk. 'Scotch on the rocks. How's that?'

Raising his glass a moment later Hooky said, 'There's a tag somewhere about Greeks and their gifts, isn't there?'

'Timeo Danaos et dona ferentis.'

'Like I said once before, Inspector, you're a brainy bird; but of course you had the advantage of being educated. I wasted my youth in that place near Windsor.'

'No need to fear this gift, Hefferman; just a friendly noggin together.'

'Never say no to a noggin – one of my few principles. This, I take it, is by way of a softener-upper?'

'Quite right, it is. I want your help.'

'You know me, Inspector. Always ready to do anything in the sacred cause of law and order. If you've any bent coppers who need straightening just apply to me.'

'I don't deal in bent coppers, Hefferman. I don't like them. In fact I hate them almost as much as I hate private eyes. What do you know about Pools?'

'I never do them.'

'Not *the* Pools. Pools the place. Pools Cottage.'

'Isn't that the place where some china was stolen recently?'

'Fancy you knowing that!'

'I read about it in the *Courier*, Inspector. It said that the police were actually pursuing enquiries in the matter so of course I didn't expect to hear any more about it.'

'Have you ever been there?'

'Inspector, I cannot tell a lie. I have never been inside

Pools Cottage in my life.'

'At least one of those statements isn't true. Is there a gate at the bottom of the drive?'

'Now, how would I know about that?'

'You might have noticed yesterday evening when you were driving by.'

'Was I driving by yesterday evening?'

'You were. Around nine o'clock as far as I can make out. In the dark anyway. Would you care to tell me where you had been?'

'Why should I? Has Orwell's nightmare really come true? Are we bound to tell Big Brother everything about ourselves?'

'If you weren't doing anything unlawful what's the harm in telling?'

Hooky shook his head sorrowfully. 'You're an unromantic type, Inspector. You've got a bureaucratic soul stuffed with official statistics and enquiries. Yesterday evening I was on my way back from a delicate matter of the heart; I had been visiting a charming young lady living in rural seclusion who sought instruction in the arts of love – what more need I say?' In effect Hooky was careful not to say anything more of any substance and he shortly took his leave.

What he had told the inspector was entirely untrue; Marsh might suspect as much, but he couldn't be sure of it. He talked the matter over with Sergeant Wilson.

'It's likely enough,' Wilson said, referring to Hooky's final remarks, 'it's a case of lock up everything feminine in sight with that character roaming around.'

'I'm not concerned with the man's morals,' Marsh replied sharply, 'even supposing he has any; what I'm worrying about is those pieces of china. At the moment I can't see any logic in it, but I've got one of those feelings about it which beat logic all ends up.'

After a moment's thought Wilson shook his head. 'Can't see it,' he said, 'it doesn't add up to me.'

'Get Chalky White in,' the inspector suggested, 'and let's hear him again about the time the stuff was taken.'

Chalky was summoned and would have embarked on a sad saga about Percy Allen's interruption of what should have been a splendid shepherds-pie, beer, and Cheddar cheese evening, but Marsh rudely cut him short.

'Never mind about all that, Chalky. We know you don't starve yourself. What had Mrs Clancy to tell you about whoever it was who took the stuff?'

The meagre details were repeated: a young woman, tall; wearing trousers; her eyes obscured by dark glasses.

Again Sergeant Wilson shook his head. 'Thin,' was his verdict.

'You couldn't identify on that; it could apply to dozens.'

Marsh nodded his agreement and after a pause said, 'It could apply to the woman who was murdered, of course; to Tessa Fellingham; and after all, she was in the antiques business.'

'Chalky says he questioned her and she told him she never dealt in china.'

'Well, she would tell him that, wouldn't she? I daresay it was true, but she would almost certainly know somebody who did deal in it. Suppose she decided to take the stuff and then flog it to another dealer who wouldn't ask where it came from?'

'How does the Romeo at the Ram come into it?'

'I see the scenario going something like this,' Marsh continued, 'this couple at Otter Lodge are having a pretty thin time trying to sell antiques. We've evidence that Hadleigh complained more than once in the Ram about business being bad. The motorist who got lost and stopped at Pools Cottage to ask her way was in fact Tessa Fellingham. During the incident, whatever it was exactly, with the cat and the parrot she saw the china figures and recognised them as being good.

'Possibly she tried to buy them, but we know from what Mrs Clancy told Chalky White that she was dead against selling anything so the Fellingham girl, if she was the one involved, decided as she couldn't buy the china figures she would steal them. She puts the idea up to Hadleigh who says he draws the line at stealing and turns it down. The girl flies off the handle at this and they have a row, and there's evidence of that, too, from the Ram. It isn't difficult to imagine the sort of thing they may say to one another; Hadleigh tells her she's a b.f. to stick her neck out by stealing and she says he never did have any guts and she always knew it.

'A few days later she calmly announces that she has pulled the trick off by herself and that the china figures are on the premises, waiting for disposal. That sends him berserk and they have a final flare-up in which she gets killed.'

Sergeant Wilson considered this for a couple of minutes before saying, 'It hangs together. It makes sense. It's possible. But the strangling seems a bit odd.'

'Copy killing, like you suggested. He knew about the Dolly Winter strangling and it seemed a good idea to him.'

'And Hefferman?'

'I can't figure out his part in things – yet; but I feel it in my bones that he's mixed up in it somehow. Maybe Hadleigh told him about the china and Hefferman didn't want to see a drinking companion get into worse trouble than he was in already so he put the stuff back himself. One thing you can be certain of – if a private eye gets mixed up in things he'll make himself as awkward as possible.'

Eileen's cousin, Connie, was surprised to see her visitor.

'It's not your usual day for looking in for a cup of tea,' she said.

'No. Well, I just felt like slipping down and seeing you. I felt I had to come.'

Domestic quarrels and family feuds were meat and drink to Connie, and from Eileen's tone of voice she scented one here.

'I'll just put the kettle on and make a pot,' she said, 'and then we can settle down to a good talk.'

Connie had never been married, Eileen had never got any pleasure out of marriage, and for a long time now the two women had shared a common theme – the unsatisfactory nature of husbands generally and of Campbell Hudson in particular.

Connie poured out two cups of tea, villainously strong stuff, and pushed the sugar bowl across.

'I ought not to,' Eileen said, helping herself to three lumps. 'What about my figure?'

'Go on. Enjoy yourself whilst you can. That's my motto. If you don't spoil yourself nobody else will. What's the matter? It's him I suppose.'

She should have said 'hope' rather than 'suppose'; she was all ears to hear some story about domestic trouble.

'I don't know what to make of it.'

'Tell me.'

'You know every Tuesday and Friday he goes to this gymnasium, O'Donovan's.'

Connie nodded.

'Well, he *hasn't* been going there. O'Donovan came into the shop today, I'd never seen him before, wanting to know if anything had happened to Campbell and saying he hadn't seen him at the gymnasium for weeks.'

'Where has he been?'

'He wouldn't tell me. He says the Lord tells him where to go.'

The two women stared at one another and eventually Connie said, 'Well, he must go *somewhere*.'

'He says he just walks about in the streets.'

'You don't believe that, do you?'

'I don't know what to believe.'

'He must be visiting somebody – another woman.'

'He always says he isn't interested in women; he's never shown much interest in me.'

'Men who say they aren't interested are always the worst, that's well known. Haven't you seen any suspicious signs? Letters, or anything like that?'

'No, nothing. Not really.'

'Well, he must have been going somewhere,' Connie repeated. 'All this business about the Lord doesn't mean a thing. Men go on like that when they want to hide something; and they've all got something to hide; every one of them. Thank goodness I never let one of them talk me into anything. I can't be made a fool of, anyway. You must have noticed something, surely?'

Eileen stirred her tea thoughtfully for some seconds and then said, 'Well, there was this Barwold business.'

'What Barwold business?'

'This man who came in one day when Campbell was out, wanting to see him and asking did he ever get as far afield as Barwold.'

'What man?'

'I don't know *what* man, Connie; *a* man. But he was very well spoken and polite, which not everybody is who comes into the shop, I can tell you. I took to him.'

'That husband of yours will have to be worrying about you soon!'

'Don't be silly, the man's only been in once.'

'And has Campbell been going to Barwold?'

'I asked him and he said he had never been there in his life.'

'Barwold? Isn't that the place where the girl Dolly Winter came from, the one who was murdered in Wardle Gardens?'

Eileen, who had followed the case avidly in the *Courier*, nodded.

'Yes, and she was buried there.'

'She was one of these girls who put cards outside the newspaper shops, wasn't she?'

'Not outside our shop. Campbell won't allow it. I tell him he's silly to turn away good money but when they ask him he always says no.'

'I expect he reckons the Lord tells him to say no. I wonder if Dolly Winter ever asked him? Has the man who spoke about Barwold ever been in again?'

'Not yet. He might do some day. I rather hope he will.'

CHAPTER THIRTEEN

Hove

My dear nephew,
  Thank you for your scarcely decipherable
letter. Presumably you were not taught handwriting at Eton, in fact I have yet to discover
what you were taught there. I'm glad you went to
see Harry Fellingham; I only hope that when you
did so you restrained your usual facetious
manner.
  I suppose this dreadful business of Tessa will
never be satisfactorily cleared up now. I haven't
as much faith in the police as I once had; there's
probably some simple fact staring them in the
face which they can't see. The entire detective
force should be composed of women; intuition is
more reliable than logic and feelings beat finger
prints any day.

Your affectionate aunt,
Theresa Page-Foley

Mrs Dawson watched Hooky reading his letter and when
he laid it down ventured to ask, 'Not another rap over the
knuckles from the head mistress I hope, Mr Hefferman?'
  'Not this time, Mrs D. Just a gentle reminder about the
deficiency of my handwriting, but otherwise words of
wisdom from on high. My aunt knows Tessa Fellingham's
father, you see, so she's very upset over the affair.'

'We are all upset by it,' Mrs Dawson avowed, 'and although Chalky White keeps telling us that the police are doing all they can I can't see that it amounts to much.'

What Inspector Marsh was doing was feeling frustrated at not getting anywhere in his murder enquiries and simultaneously harbouring a strong resentment against Hooky over the affair of the restored china figures. The Inspector felt convinced that Hooky had a hand in putting the figures back, but he realised that it was going to be impossible to prove it.

If Hooky had a hand in putting the china back it was pretty obvious that he must be more involved in the whole Tessa Fellingham-Hadleigh business than he had owned up to. Marsh resented this, and said so strongly to Sergeant Wilson.

'I wish he'd clear out, Wilson, and go back to that pornographic patch of his in Soho.'

'He says the Cotswold air suits him, sir; he says he likes it here.'

'We'll have to do our best to cure that. I'll have him in for questioning again and you tell Chalky White to lean on him in every possible way; anything to do with that car of his – suspicion of driving under the influence – anything as long as we make ourselves a nuisance to him.'

Mrs Dawson noticed the new frequent police attentions to Hooky and commented on them. 'That Chalky White seems to be making an awful nuisance of himself, Mr Hefferman, just as though he had some sort of grudge against you.'

Hooky laughed easily. 'Chalky's all right, Mrs D,' he said. 'He's not a bad chap at all; it's his boss who doesn't like me. Inspector Marsh is convinced that I've had something to do with all the dark deeds that have gone on round here.'

Good Mrs Dawson was shocked. 'That's nonsense,' she announced stoutly, 'how can the silly man possibly think that?'

'He's just got a feeling about me. And my aunt says that feelings are all important, she says they beat finger prints any day.'

Martha Dawson was intrigued. 'Feelings are funny things,' she allowed. 'I had a feeling once about a ghost. Mind you, I don't really believe in ghosts. Never have done. But all the same just this once I had this funny feeling about one; you can't explain it, can you? Have you ever had a feeling, Mr Hefferman?'

'Yes, not long ago. Just for a few seconds a very queer feeling. In the churchyard here.'

'In the churchyard! Oh dear, that *is* creepy. Did you see something, then?'

'I saw a man standing over a freshly dug grave, staring down at it. Staring down at the grave of Dolly Winter, that girl who was murdered. He wasn't one of the family. He was a stranger and he was standing there staring down at the grave.'

'I wonder why he was doing that,' Mrs Dawson said.

Hooky wondered, too. He wondered a great deal about little newsagent Hudson. He had a golden rule for solving difficulties – when in doubt get it down on paper. In his bedroom at the Ram he listed – on the back of an envelope – the things he knew about Hudson.

1. Hudson had been looking at Otter Lodge and had been told to 'sod off' by Tessa on the day Dolly Winter was buried.

2. Hudson had been standing over Dolly Winter's grave, staring at it.

3. Hudson had denied knowing anything about Dolly Winter.

4. Mrs Hudson had said that her husband never went to Barwold.

5. Hooky himself had seen Hudson's car in Barwold on the day Tessa Fellingham was murdered.

Five curious little pieces of fact which didn't quite fit into a pattern yet. 'Maybe they never will,' Hooky thought. 'Maybe there isn't a pattern – but it's worth trying to find out.'

His plan was to find Mrs Hudson in the shop when her husband wasn't there, and this involved a certain amount of watching and waiting. Tedious work, but work Hooky was well used to since watching and waiting formed a large part of the humdrum side of P.I. business – waiting and watching to report on what time the errant husband left his mistress's flat; waiting and watching to see which restaurant the naughty wife was taken to by her lover; to keep tally on exactly which directors went to the secret meeting of the board; to tell the angry millionaire whether his son was still frequenting the West End gambling places or not.

For all these things you waited, watched, made your report and drew your fee. Run of the mill P.I. work. None of it glamorous, but sometimes amusing; even dangerous at times when subjects turned nasty.

So, taking himself to Dunsly, Hooky put the Jag in the big car park behind the Regent Cinema and went on foot to North Street.

Hudson's car was standing outside the newsagent's shop so Hooky took up a strategic position in a nearby doorway and waited. After a boring half-hour the gods were kind. Hudson came out of his shop, got into his car and drove off.

The car had scarcely reached the end of the street before Hooky was smiling in his most disarming fashion across the counter at Mrs Hudson. Eileen remembered the end of her conversation with Connie – *has the man who spoke about Barwold ever been in again? Not yet. He might do some day. I rather hope he will* – and here he was, as masculine looking as ever. Eileen felt a little flustered, pleasantly flustered.

To give some substance to his visit Hooky bought a copy of *The Times* and then asked, 'Mr Hudson about?'

'I'm afraid he's just gone out.'

'Off on some business, I suppose.'

'He's gone to the wholesalers; we're always having trouble with them.'

'You must get a lot of worries in your line of business, Mrs Hudson – it is Mrs Hudson, isn't it?'

'Yes, that's right. Eileen Hudson.'

'That's a pretty name – Eileen. Everybody calls me Hooky – well, you can see why, can't you?'

Eileen laughed. She never dared to laugh at her husband, but this man seemed to be the sort you could laugh at and he wouldn't mind. She screwed up her courage to ask him, 'Excuse me, but do you come from Barwold?'

'I'm staying there for the present, yes.'

'Last time you came in you asked if Mr Hudson ever went there.'

'Does he?'

'He says he never does.'

Hooky smiled at Eileen Hudson, a slow conspiratorial smile which did exactly what it was intended to do. It conveyed the message *we all know about husbands and the things they say, don't we*, and it encouraged her to ask, 'I was wondering if you have ever seen him there?'

'I was there the day that girl Dolly Winter was buried.'

The name of the murdered woman created a silence in the small shop. Eileen Hudson stared wonderingly at the man who had uttered it and he looked steadily back at her. All of a sudden there was inexplicable tension in the air and Eileen realised that there were depths here she did well to be afraid of. But as well as being afraid she was excited. A host of confused ideas made her uncertain what next to say. She was saved from saying anything by Hooky's question. 'Did Dolly Winter ever come into this shop?'

'She might have done,' Eileen answered slowly. 'She was one of those girls who put up cards, wasn't she? But Campbell won't have anything to do with them. He hates them.'

A customer came in, a large talkative woman with three noisy children wanting postcards and sweets.

Hooky left; whatever spell there had been was broken and was unlikely to be renewed. He walked thoughtfully back to the Regent car park. It seemed to him that he had learnt something, but he was not sure how much; one phrase stayed in his mind and the vehemence with which it had been spoken, '*he hates them*'.

When the talkative woman and her three children left Eileen experienced a sharp attack of a feeling which was no novelty for her – intense annoyance that her cousin Connie was not on the telephone. She was bursting to tell Connie about Hooky's visit with its disturbing question about Dolly Winter; indeed she felt the urge to do this so strongly that she was tempted to do an unheard-of thing. She was tempted to put up the *Closed* notice and leave the shop locked up for an hour; but second thoughts made her realise the danger in this. Campbell would be sure to find out and every sort of unpleasant complication would ensue. Reluctantly she abandoned the idea, and contented herself with registering a firm intention of slipping down to see Connie later in the day, whatever Campbell might say.

When Hudson came back from his visit to the wholesaler Eileen shot a quick, speculative look at him. Nowadays it was very seldom that she consciously studied the face of the man she was married to. He was there; part of life; inescapable; too customary a thing to warrant more than the most cursory glance; but now she did take a close searching look at him, curious to see what expression would show on the face of a man who was living a secret life of his own, who probably had a mistress somewhere and possibly other unthinkable entanglements as well. As usual it was impossible to tell from Hudson's face what he was really thinking about; Eileen wondered angrily whether it was equally impossible to tell from his words what he had really been doing.

'Did you sort things out with the wholesaler?' she asked, not so much because she wanted to hear the answer as because she wanted to make him say something.

153

'More or less. Has anybody been in?'

'A woman and three kids. Sweets and postcards.'

'Nobody else?'

'No, nobody.'

But Hudson's quick, surveying eye had already spotted something. 'When I went out,' he said, 'there was one copy of *The Times* left, now it's gone. Did the sweets and postcards woman buy it?'

'No, she didn't.'

'Then somebody else has been in?'

'Yes, a man. I'd forgotten for the moment. A man came in and asked for *The Times*. I'd forgotten.'

'A regular?'

'No. Not a regular. I don't know who he was.'

Hudson considered for a moment and then seemed satisfied; Eileen, watching him closely, devoutly hoped that he was. Conjuring up a quick, bright tone of voice she said, 'I think I'll slip down and have a cup of tea with Connie this afternoon.'

'Whatever do you want to go and see her for?'

'It's nice to have a talk with somebody.'

'Talk?'

'Well, *we* never do, do we?'

'I've too many things to think about to bother with talk,' Hudson announced. His wife said nothing, but she wondered what those things were.

'That man has been in again, Connie; the one who asked about Barwold.'

'My dear! Tell me.'

'Campbell was out at the wholesalers, so I was on my own.'

'Lucky you. What happened?'

'Nothing *happened*, Connie; nothing happened, but—'

'But what?'

'Well, for one thing he said he thought Eileen was a pretty name.'

154

'And you're telling me nothing happened! What else did he say?'

'He talked about Dolly Winter again.'

'Why about her? What had he got to say about her?'

'He was in Barwold the day she was buried there.' Eileen paused before adding, 'And do you know, Connie, I believe Campbell was there that day, too. Somehow I believe that.'

The two women stared at one another and at last Connie asked slowly, 'Why ever should he have been?'

Eileen shook her head. 'I don't know. I can't explain it; but you get a feeling about these things at times, don't you? The man said his name was Hooky.'

'Hooky? That's a funny sort of a name.'

'It's because of his broken nose, I suppose. He asked if Dolly Winter had ever been into the shop about putting up one of her cards.'

'And had she?'

'I don't know.'

'Campbell would know, if you asked him, wouldn't he?'

Hooky drove back to Barwold slowly and in contemplative mood. His thoughts about the visit to the North Street shop kept alternating. At one moment he was congratulating himself on having almost unearthed something, at the next he was telling himself that 'almost' was the significant word; and 'almost' wasn't good enough; 'almost' meant that he hadn't really got hold of any hard facts at all; all he had got was atmosphere, feelings. Feelings beat finger prints every time, the Epistle from On High had declared; it might be true, of course, the old lady from Hove had a habit of being right, and Hooky's feeling was a strong one – '*he hates them*'. Hooky remembered the venom of the words and reflected that people who cultivated hatreds were apt to be fanatics and that fanatics were worth watching.

Things were slack in the bar of the Ram that evening and for want of somebody to talk to Hooky drew out the copy of *The Times* he had bought in Dunsly and began to study the crossword.

Mrs Dawson watched him with interest. 'I've never tried one of those things,' she said. 'I can never understand them. They flummox me.'

'You're not the only one, Mrs D,' Hooky assured her, 'but if you peg away you usually get somewhere in the end.'

A desultory game of darts was in progress; Hooky was invited to take part but declined; talk turned to the subject of the mysteriously returned pieces of china; this was now treated as a joke more than anything else, although one wiseacre shook his head and declared, 'There's something queer there, you can depend upon it; it's got old Chalky White puzzled anyway.' Amid general laughter it was agreed that it wouldn't take much to puzzle old Chalky.

Not being busy serving, Mrs Dawson enquired how Hooky was faring with 'that crossword thing'.

Hooky replied that the man who compiled it evidently had a tortuous mind, but that it was fun unravelling the knots. Mrs Dawson leant across and somewhat tentatively read out a clue – 'It sounds as though the cooler is at the top of the house, what a dangerous fellow.'

'Now what on earth does that mean?' the honest woman demanded. 'The only thing at the top of this house is the attic.'

'Mrs D, you're a genius,' Hooky declared, 'the very word I'm looking for. A fan is a cooler, isn't it, and the attic is at the top – *fanatic*.'

'So I've got one right, have I?' Mrs Dawson cried in delighted astonishment.

'You have indeed. I expect you'd do the whole thing in ten minutes.'

'But what does that bit about a dangerous fellow mean?'

'Wouldn't you agree that a fanatic can be dangerous?'

'I can't abide fanatics. Never could. Especially the religious sort. There used to be a lot in Dunsly and round about as reckoned they were the Elect People or Select People, something like that. My father always used to say they were the blindest, most intolerant collection he ever knew. Yes, I suppose a fanatic could be dangerous.'

'Dangerous enough to kill?'

Martha Dawson gave a little shudder. 'There's been enough talk of killing in Barwold, Mr Hefferman,' she said.

I didn't like the idea of Terry O'Donovan coming to the shop and asking about me. I didn't like it one bit. I confess it shook me. It was something I hadn't bargained for, and it made me suddenly realise that however safe you thought yourself danger could always be lurking in all sorts of unexpected places. Rather to my surprise Eileen didn't go on about it too much; she wanted to know where I had been going instead of to the gymnasium and whether she believed what I told her or not I don't know. Probably not. Plain, simple truth doesn't mean a thing to people like Eileen. They live in a fantasy, TV world. She can't get this idea of another woman out of her head; but, as I say, she didn't go on about it too much, she let it drop. At any rate outwardly. But I could see her wrapping the thing up inside her head, putting it on one side to gloat over, like a dog with a bone; probably to talk over with that cousin of hers. That's her way, of course; she never has anything out in the open; she keeps things to herself and broods over them. And that might make her dangerous. I didn't like it.

But when a few days had gone by I began to think that it didn't matter too much after all. If I didn't want to go to O'Donovan's why should I? And how could Eileen possibly guess the real reason why I had given up going? If the police hadn't been able to pin anything on me I didn't think the stupid woman I was married to could, and I had made up my mind already that it wouldn't pay her to try.

It's strange when people won't believe the truth. You tell the truth and people – stupid, TV fed people like Eileen – don't believe it; it isn't good enough for them. 'What did you do instead of going to O'Donovan's?' 'I walked about in the streets,' you say, and you get an unbelieving look, a you-can't-fool-me-I-know-better-than-that look.

But I enjoyed walking through the streets, thinking how different I was from all the other people; the ordinary people. I knew I wasn't ordinary. I was one of the Elect. The Lord gave me work to do and I did it.

I got into the habit of stopping outside other newsagents' shops and studying the card advertisements they put up. Not the second-hand dishwasher for sale and the baby-sitter urgent wanted sort; not that lot, but the cards put up by the prostitutes and paid for, as I know, at 40p a week. Sometimes there would be three, or even four, cards in the window and I felt like going inside and telling the shopkeeper that the money he was getting for them was immoral, he was living on the earnings of whores.

One day I was looking at the cards in the window of the big shop in Station Drive, where they must do three times the business we do in North Street, when a girl came out whom I recognised. And after a quick look she recognised me.

'You haven't been up to Colin Avenue yet,' she said. 'Still thinking about it?'

I shook my head.

'Having a good read of the cards you're too damned holy to put up yourself?' she asked. I told her I didn't put up the cards of the likes of her because the Lord told me not to.

'The Lord tells me I've got to eat,' she said, 'and I can't eat unless I earn my living, which is what you damned do-gooders want to stop me doing.'

I wasn't going to argue with a common whore about what the Lord told me to do and I would have turned away except that I suddenly remembered what the detective sergeant had said about asking the girl if she had known Dolly Winter.

The truth is, of course, that those two words, that name Dolly Winter, was constantly in my mind lying just below the level of consciousness; in a way the words almost spoke themselves.

She hesitated for a moment and looked a bit closely at me, then she said, 'Yes, I knew Dolly; why are you asking about her?'

'If you were friendly with her you ought to go to the police; they want to talk to anybody who knew her.'

'I suppose the Lord tells you to get mixed up with the police,' the girl said. 'Well, he doesn't tell me to; he tells me to avoid the bastards like the plague.'

I walked away from Station Drive feeling oddly excited. Seeing that whore again and speaking Dolly Winter's name had disturbed me. 'I suppose the Lord tells you to get mixed up with the police,' the girl had said, and turning her words over in my mind the idea came to me that maybe she was nearer the truth than she could possibly have known. What I had done to Dolly Winter had been the Lord's business and the Lord wouldn't want me to get into trouble for it, and probably the best way of avoiding trouble was to keep in touch with the police and to make that detective sergeant think that I was doing all I could to help him. Surely the man who had committed a murder was the least likely person to walk into a police station and talk about it?

Going there was all part of the excitement that was bubbling in me, it put an edge on things; it was like walking a tight rope; there was danger, but I knew I was too clever for it to hurt me. So I didn't go straight back from Station Drive to North Street; in her semi-efficient way Eileen could go on looking after the shop a little longer. Perhaps Terry O'Donovan would come in again, I thought, or somebody else she could gossip with about me.

I turned away from the North Street direction and made my way to the police station. When I asked for Sergeant Wilson I was told I was lucky, he had been out on a job all morning but had just got back. Whether he was surprised to see me or not I don't know, but he was friendy enough.

'Let's see, Mr Hudson, isn't it?' he asked.

'That's right.'

'How's business in North Street?'

'Much as usual. I've seen that girl again.'

'Which girl is that, then?'

'The whore from Colin Avenue.'

'Don't tell me you've been going up to Colin Avenue, Mr Hudson?'

The stupid question and the way he laughed when he asked it annoyed me. 'That isn't funny,' I told him. 'I don't go in for that sort of thing. I don't mix with women like that. I hate them.'

'No, no; of course not,' he went on quickly, and I think he saw that he had said the wrong thing. 'This is the same girl who came into your shop wanting you to put up a card, is that right?'

'Yes. And I refused. The Lord doesn't want me to make a living like that.'

'And what did you want to tell me about her?'

'You asked me to find out if any of these girls knew Dolly Winter; well, this one did and I asked her and she told me yes, she knew Dolly Winter.'

Dolly Winter, Dolly Winter – I need not have said the name twice but the truth is I was getting a wonderful feeling of superiority out of sitting there in the police station, in the headquarters of the enemy as you might say, and talking with the thick-witted policeman about the murder I had committed and which he would never be able to bring home to me.

'Did she tell you anything about the murdered woman?' the sergeant asked.

'No. Just that she knew her. She just said she knew Dolly Winter.'

The sergeant wrote something on a piece of paper on his desk, and thought for a moment, tapping his biro against his front teeth, then he asked, 'Anything else?'

'No, that's all.'

'Well, thank you very much for coming in, Mr Hudson. Every little helps. We'll chase it up.'

'You're getting on with the case, then?' I asked. 'But no

one has been arrested yet, have they?'

'Not yet. But if public-spirited people like yourself keep coming in with bits of information we shall get somewhere in time.'

'Let's hope so,' I said, 'we ratepayers want to see something for our money.'

I went away from the police station well pleased with myself. Things couldn't have gone better. 'Public-spirited,' the sergeant had called me, and it was perfectly true – much truer than the plodding Wilson could possibly have guessed – I *was* public-spirited, there were too many whores in the world, mocking the Lord, and I was helping to get rid of them.

I felt too exhilarated to go straight back to the shop so instead, in Culvert Street, I did something I hardly ever did in daytime; I turned into a pub, the Lamb and Flag.

I knew it by sight, but I had never been in it before. Inside it looked bright and cheerful, and that's how my mood was at the moment so it suited me.

I ordered half a pint of bitter and the barman gave up reading his paper just long enough to serve me.

'Terrible thing these burgularies,' he said. 'There are two or three in the paper every day. I don't know what the police are doing.'

'Being fooled to the top of their bent,' I told him happily, and he looked at me a bit oddly so that I thought maybe it was rather a foolish thing to say and I said no more and began sipping my half pint.

There weren't many people in the bar and I noticed a couple, a man and a woman sitting at a table by one of the windows. She had a glass of port in front of her and he was drinking a Guinness which was just about right, I reckoned, for what they looked like – a whore with a client she had picked up in the street.

I wondered if, in the bedroom, he would feel afterwards as long ago I had felt with the woman of the Elect People, as I had felt not so long ago with that other one when I saw

161

her standing by her car in the Barwold lane. That was the day when the MP should have come to hear what we had to say at the newsagents' meeting but didn't turn up. I could have gone back to the shop but I didn't. I suppose you might say that I *should* have gone back to the shop; but I had other things to think about. I was thinking, as usual, about Barwold. On the way there I stopped for a sandwich at a pub and the girl in tight trousers served me. She obviously didn't think much of me – well, people don't always know whom they are talking to, do they?

In Barwold, in the churchyard, the clergyman saw me looking at the grave, Dolly Winter's grave. 'Tragic, isn't it?' he said, and, just to humour him, I agreed. 'Yes, tragic,' but of course 'tragic' wasn't what I thought. I thought it was splendid, something to exult over; the hand of the Lord had struck and I had been His agent. I didn't go about in a flapping white surplice mouthing plummy platitudes, I did the Lord's work quietly and efficiently.

I was half hoping to meet the chap they call Hooky, half hoping that I wouldn't. I couldn't make up my mind about that man; on the surface he seemed friendly enough but I had a feeling there was something there which might be dangerous to me.

I went along to the end of the village and stood outside the antiques shop just as I had done on the day of the funeral. But this time it was closed and the woman I was thinking about didn't come out all but naked and say something to me as she had done that first time.

If the Lord doesn't want me to see the woman, I thought, that's his affair and I've got to accept it.

There was now no reason for being in Barwold so I turned away from Otter Lodge and made my way back to where I had left the car, hidden away in a side lane. I was feeling a bit flat. I had been so certain of an impulse inside me which had said 'go to Barwold' and then, when I got there, I couldn't see any reason for going; there was nothing.

I had left the village some ten minutes behind me when the lane dipped between high banks and the trees arched greenly overhead; at the corner, where the lane turned, a car was drawn up and a woman was standing by it. When I saw who she was I knew why the Lord had sent me to Barwold.

'Thank goodness you've come,' she said. 'I was beginning to think there was nobody left in the world – oh, it's you is it? What are you doing in these parts? Well, never mind that. Do you know anything about cars? Mine's packed up completely. I'll have to get Turley's to look at it but I've got to get there first.'

Turley's was the big, fashionable, garage in Dunsly, not far from North Street actually, where presumably she had her car serviced.

My heart had already quickened its beat and I could feel the pulses throbbing in my ears, but I answered her quietly enough.

'I'll have a look at it and see what I can do,' I told her.

'Bless you, you funny little man,' she said in that irritating, high-pitched voice of hers, 'I knew you'd come in useful some day.'

I said nothing to that. I got out of my car and stood by hers, close to her. Now all feeling of flatness had vanished. Now I felt alive, tingling with excitement to the tips of the strong fingers I would so soon be using. Now the spittle was dry in my throat. If an earthquake had happened then I don't think I would have noticed it. She repeated her question, 'What are you doing in these parts? What brings you to Barwold again?'

'The Lord's business,' I told her, and, not realising that it was her death sentence, she answered in her usual flippant way, 'Well, I must remember to give the Lord a vote of thanks next time I meet him for sending you along. I expect you know all about cars, do you?'

'I'll see what I can do,' I repeated, and my voice sounded strange to me so I don't know what it must have sounded

163

like to her.

I was standing close to her now and the smell and the femininity of her disturbed me profoundly.

'It was going along perfectly all right,' she said, 'no trouble at all, and then all of a sudden, out of the blue, the damned thing packed up.'

Those were the last words she spoke. I whipped round suddenly and hit her hard in the face, a sort of short arm jab. It all but stunned her and before she could recover I had my hands round her neck and I was squeezing the life out of her. . . .

That's how it happened that afternoon in the lonely lane near Barwold and now, in the Lamb and Flag, sipping my modest half pint, looking at the couple sitting by the window, I remembered it all; I remembered every terrible, sickening, glorious minute.

The barman was saying something to me. I couldn't make out what, I wasn't tuned in to the present. I don't know exactly what I said to him in reply, but it was so off-beam that he looked at me oddly again. He evidently thought I was a queer fish, a bit of a nutter maybe. I finished up my drink quickly and went out before he came to any more conclusions.

I walked slowly back towards North Street. I didn't like the way that barman had looked at me. I told myself I was being silly and that there was nothing to worry about, and I almost convinced myself. But not quite. Coming away from the police station I had felt a sort of euphoria. Now all that had suddenly gone, evaporated. I told myself not to be a fool, not to get worried just because the barman in a strange pub thought I was a bit of an odd fish.

But I was worrying about other things besides the barman.

I had been beginning to think that the business of not going to O'Donovan's gym had died down and that Eileen wasn't worrying about it any more, but of course it's silly to think like that about a woman, especially one like Eileen;

164

she doesn't get many ideas into her head and when she does get one she never lets it go.

It's true she hadn't said anything more about O'Donovan's but then, after a day or two, there was that business of the *Times*.

I had come back from the wholesaler's and asked the usual questions – anyone been in? Any business?

'A woman and three children,' Eileen told me. 'Postcards, sweets; nobody else.'

But because I'm sharp-eyed and know what I've got in the shop I wanted to know about the last copy of *The Times* which had been in the rack when I went out and wasn't there any longer.

Oh yes, she said. There *had* been someone else in; a man who bought *The Times*; she had forgotten him.

I didn't believe her. I didn't tell her so, but I didn't believe her. I didn't think she had forgotten. I thought she hadn't wanted me to know about the man coming in. She was hiding something and I wondered what it was. Was the man who bought *The Times* the same one who had asked if I ever got as far afield as Barwold, I wondered. I didn't like it. I didn't want Eileen to start thinking about Barwold. . . .

'That chap Hudson has been in again,' Sergeant Wilson said.

'Hudson?'

'The newspaper shop in North Street.'

'I wish all newspapers and their editors and their owners were at the bottom of the sea,' Marsh declared fervently; the *Evening Courier* had lately been running a series about the inefficiency of the local police force and the inspector's opinion of the press was at a low ebb.

'What did he want?'

'The funny thing is that's exactly what I've been asking myself ever since he left.'

'Didn't he tell you?'

'He said he had seen this pro who works in Colin Avenue

165

and asked her if she had known Dolly Winter and she said yes she did know her and he had come in to tell us.'

'Well, you asked him to, didn't you?'

'Yes, I did.'

'There you are then – public-spirited citizen (don't make me laugh) responds to police request for help, that's the sort of news item I'd like to see in the *Courier*.'

'That's what I told him he was, public-spirited, and he loved it.'

'What are you worrying about, then?'

Wilson shook his head. 'There's something wrong about that chap. I think he's a bit off beam, unbalanced. I think he likes coming in here. He gets some sort of a kick out of it. In some way or other it makes him feel smart, pleased with himself. He won't put the girls' cards up in his window but I've a feeling he spends quite a bit of time thinking about them.'

'Lives by fantasies, eh? I wonder if he himself ever knew Dolly Winter?'

When I got back to the shop I found there had been quite a little flurry of business whilst I had been to the police station and to the Lamb and Flag. That's how it goes in our sort of trade, nothing at all for maybe an hour and then three or four people in all at once. Eileen seemed to have coped all right. When she had finished telling me about it she added at the end, casually, 'And Connie popped in for a minute or two,' She knew I wouldn't like that. I didn't like Eileen 'slipping down' to see her cousin, or her cousin 'popping in' to see her.

'What did she want?' I asked.

'She'd been shopping and she just looked in for a chat. She asked how you were.'

This last bit was by way of a sop; Eileen knew my views about the shop, it was a place for doing business, not for having cosy family chats. I wondered what they had chatted about. Me probably, I supposed, and the short-

166

comings of husbands generally; well, that was harmless enough.

Then Eileen suddenly said, 'Connie was talking about Barwold,' and I realised from the change in her tone of voice that this was really the essence of what she wanted to say. Barwold – I pricked up my ears; this wasn't harmless at all, this could be dangerous and I didn't intend to let this silly chattering woman be dangerous to me.

'Barwold? I said. 'Why was she talking about Barwold?'

'She wanted to know if I had ever been there.'

I said nothing, but just looked at the woman, the thin and scrawny woman with the thin and scrawny neck.

'Have *you* ever been there?' Eileen asked.

I still said nothing, and misreading my silence she plucked up the rest of her courage to ask, 'Were you there the day Dolly Winter was buried?'

I continued to stare at her, and at that thin and scrawny neck.

CHAPTER FOURTEEN

'You remember what I was saying the other day, boss, about that chap Hudson, about his being a bit of a nutter, a fanatic?'

'As far as I can see that applies to most citizens of this town; what's new about Hudson?'

'I saw him this morning.'

'You went to see him again?'

'No. It was in Station Drive. He didn't know I was coming along and there he was staring into the window of that big newsagents' shop where they've got a windowful of cards put up – interesting homework sought by enthusiastic blonde and all the rest of it, you know the sort of thing.'

'Hudson wouldn't be the only man to have a read of them,' Marsh said.

'No. But for somebody who hates the whole thing – well, I got the impression that in a way it's something he loves to hate, that he feeds on his hatred of it; and I'll tell you another thing about him, he's given up going to O'Donovan's.'

'The gymnasium? Used he to go there?'

'He was one of Terry O'Donovan's regulars, apparently. Terry says for a small man he's very strongly built, and muscular, with especially powerful hands. He went regularly twice a week for a long time and then suddenly stopped. No notice, nothing said about giving up, he just didn't come any more.'

'Why was that?'

Wilson shook his head. 'I'll tell you *when* it was,' he said.

'He gave up going there the week after the Dolly Winter murder.'

The inspector tapped his pencil against his teeth reflectively for a few seconds and then asked, 'Any connection?'

'Who knows, boss? But I'm going to call on Mr Campbell Hudson with his twisted mind and his strong hands and ask him again if he ever knew Dolly Winter.'

As usual Eileen was fiddling about, rearranging things. There was absolutely no need to. Everything was in order; in its place; where it should be; but that's not good enough for her; she must pick things up, consider them and in the end very probably put them down again exactly where they were. It drives me to distraction watching her and I was just about to tell her pretty sharply to stop messing about and find something useful to do when the door opened and a customer came in.

Only he wasn't a customer, he was Detective Sergeant Wilson.

'Busy?' he asked.

'There's always plenty to do,' I told him, but as a matter of fact there *wasn't* plenty to do; business was very slack, but I wasn't going to tell him that. I wondered why he had come, whether it was something I had said on my last visit to the police station that he had come about. I couldn't think of anything, and although I didn't think the police were going to be clever enough to fix anything on me I would have been happier if he hadn't come.

'I expect you've got time for a little chat, though,' he said, and I didn't like the false-friendly way in which he said it.

I caught Eileen's eye and gave a jerk of my head which meant I wanted her to clear out into the back room. I knew, of course, that when she was there she would do her best to eavesdrop, but it wasn't altogether easy and she certainly wouldn't be able to hear everything.

169

The detective stopped her going. 'Don't send Mrs Hudson away,' he said. 'It's all in the family, isn't it? And, you never know, she might be able to help. I'm sure you don't have any secrets from her, do you?'

Cunning bastard, I thought, always asking questions to trip you up, to trap you. But not cunning enough to trap me.

'I haven't got any secrets from anybody,' I told him. 'What did you want to talk about?'

'Oh, this and that. A friendly chat. Have any more girls come in wanting to put up cards?'

'No, they haven't. And I wouldn't put up the cards if they had been.'

'I know you wouldn't, I know how you feel about that, Mr Hudson. Of course, other newsagents put them up, don't they?'

'I don't know. What other newsagents do is no concern of mine; they can put up the prostitutes' cards if they like, I'm not interested in them.'

'What we are interested in,' the detective said, 'is finding people who knew Dolly Winter, the girl who was murdered in Wardle Gardens; I expect you remember about that, don't you?'

I told him yes, I remembered about Wardle Gardens.

'Did Dolly Winter ever come in here, trying to put up a card?'

'Not to my knowledge.'

Eileen had been listening to this agog; anything like this was meat and drink to her; she probably imagined herself taking part in some soap opera drama on the box. The sergeant turned to her and asked if she had ever seen Dolly Winter in the shop.

'I wouldn't know her if I had,' Eileen answered, and then for some reason or other she felt prompted to say something which from her point of view was very foolish indeed. 'Wasn't she the girl who was buried at Barwold?' she asked.

'That's right,' the detective said. 'Barwold. Do you know

the place, Mrs Hudson?'

Eileen was in a fluster now. 'No, no; I don't know it, I've just heard of it, that's all. I've never been there.'

The sergeant turned to me. 'Have *you* ever been there, Mr Hudson?'

I told him I might have been through the place at one time or another. I couldn't remember.

That seemed to dispose of Barwold, at any rate for the time being, and I can't say I was sorry; but Sergeant Wilson's next question was almost as disturbing.

'Does Terry O'Donovan ever advertise in your window?'

Bringing in Terry O'Donovan's name was something new and I didn't like it. How had they got on to Terry O'Donovan? I wondered if Eileen had said something to somebody.

'The gymnasium man?' I answered. 'No, he never has done.'

'You used to go there once, is that right?'

'Yes.'

'Every Tuesday and Friday?'

'That's when I used to go.'

'And why did you stop going there, Mr Hudson?'

'I got tired of it, I suppose.'

That seemed to satisfy him. 'Ah well,' he said, 'I suppose we all get tired of things in the end. Thank you very much for your help, you and Mrs Hudson. Good day to you both.'

When he went out of the shop neither of us spoke for a minute or two. Eileen said nothing because she was scared. She had a feeling that she ought not to have mentioned Barwold and she knew that I would be wondering how the police knew about O'Donovan's. She didn't know what my reaction was going to be and she was scared.

For my part I deliberately kept silent for a couple of minutes just to let her go on being scared; to let her stew in her own juice.

So I didn't say anything straightaway, but something was already beginning to form in my mind.

171

For some reason or other Eileen was already suspicious about Barwold, and she was going to keep on nagging away at the Barwold idea, asking questions here, there and everywhere, gossiping, hinting at things – being the woman she was she would go on like that just as long as she was allowed to. Until she was stopped. And if I was going to stop her I would have to think things out carefully. I mustn't start by frightening her.

'The sergeant seemed pleased with what we were able to tell him,' I said in the most matter-of-fact friendly sort of way. 'I don't suppose he'll be coming in again because we've nothing more to tell him, but if he does, give him a cup of tea; you make a very nice cup of tea, Eileen.'

Hearing voices raised – and voices which he thought he recognised – in the street below, Hooky crossed to his bedroom window and looked out. A small comic-drama was unfolding itself in the street outside the Ram.

'Is that your dog, sir?' PC White demanded, not without a certain heat in his voice.

'You know perfectly well the dog is mine,' Lynton Hadleigh answered. 'I've bought a licence for it and everything is in order.'

There was a crisp note of assurance in Hadleigh's voice which surprised Hooky; this was a different-sounding Hadleigh from the downcast character of recent days.

'I must ask you to keep the animal under control then, sir,' Chalky White went on. 'It very nearly had me off my machine,'

'Then I suggest you learn to control your machine,' Hadleigh advised him, 'and stop blaming dumb animals,' and with a brisk nod of dismissal he turned on his heel, and accompanied by a small Jack Russell terrier went in through the front door of the Ram.

Always intrigued by any unexpected behaviour on the part of his fellow humans, Hooky left his bedroom and hastened downstairs to the bar, where Lynton Hadleigh

172

greeted him joyously. 'Just in time,' he announced. 'Mrs Dawson has gone in search of a bottle of champers so we can celebrate together – you know Midge, don't you?'

Having narrowly evaded hostile attentions from the dog on more than one occasion Hooky did indeed know the Jack Russell, which was now regarding him with all the sharp-eyed malevolence of its breed.

There were a few simple rules of conduct in life which experience had taught Hooky it was foolish to neglect; foremost among them was never criticise other people's children or dogs. Suppressing his real feelings, therefore (which would have earned him a severe reprimand from the RSPCA), he said, 'Jolly little fellow – was he getting into trouble with the law?'

'You can't blame a dog for taking a dim view of policemen,' Hadleigh answered, 'especially an intelligent dog like Midge. He knows what a confounded nuisance that oaf White has been lately, pestering me with questions all the time. Well, he won't be pestering me much longer. I'm off.'

At this point Mrs Dawson appeared carrying a bottle.

'Moet et Chandon, Mr Hadleigh,' she said, 'is that all right?'

'Two excellent fellows,' Hadleigh assured her. 'I used to know them very well at one time.'

'And the bottle's nice and cold, sir; it's beautifully cool in the cellar.'

'The ideal recipe for dinner in town,' Hadleigh said, 'always was, and always will be, a large cold bottle and a small hot bird – let me see to the cork, Mrs D.'

The cork having been seen to and the glasses filled Hooky raised his and said, 'I don't know what it is we are celebrating but here's to it, anyway.'

'What we are celebrating,' Hadleigh told him, 'is my flight into freedom. Who was it who led somebody out of somewhere into somewhere else where they would much sooner be?'

'Moses had a stab at it with the Israelites,' Hooky suggested.

Hadleigh said he doubted if any Israelites would be accompanying him, he was off on his own.

'Off? Where to?' Hooky asked. 'What's happened, old sport?'

'The business of Otter Lodge Antiques has been sold, lock stock and barrel; whatever that means; as far as I know there aren't any locks stocks or barrels in the place; but never mind, a chap from Hereford who wants to start up in the antiques business has bought the lot. The premises and everything on the premises. No argument, no arrangements, no business about "if I can fix a mortgage", nothing like that, just cash down and almost exactly what I asked for it.'

'We'll be sorry to see you go, Mr Hadleigh,' Mrs Dawson said in her friendly way.

Hadleigh reached for the bottle and replenished his glass. 'With all due respect to you, Mrs D,' he said, 'I can't say I shall be sorry to go; after all that has happened I'm glad to go. It was silly to come in the first place; silly to let myself be talked into taking up the antiques business. In your time, Hooky, have you never let yourself be talked into doing something silly by a girl?'

'Hardly ever done anything else, old sport.'

'Well, there you are then. Don't get me wrong. I'm not saying a word against Tessa. Especially after what has happened. Good God, no. Not a word against her. She was a hell of a character. Too much of a character for me, I suppose. We had plenty of fun together, but she was damned hard to live up to; and, on the whole, to get tied up with her was a mistake. I can see that now. Mind you, she probably thought it was a mistake to get tied up with me. By and large we men don't amount to much, do we, Hooky?'

'Men are unwise and curiously planned,' Hooky pointed out, adding, 'and, Mrs D, go down into that admirably cool cellar of yours, will you, and produce a second bottle, on me this time. I can see it will be needed.'

Whilst Mrs Dawson was absent Hadleigh seemed in two minds, reluctant to go on with the subject of Tessa, yet at the same time unwilling to leave it altogether.

'Do you suppose the Colonel thinks I had anything to do with what happened?' he asked.

Hooky shook his head. 'Shouldn't think so. He's a decent little chap. One of the endangered species. He's a gent.'

'Will you be seeing him again?'

'Possibly. If I get orders to.'

'Orders? Who gives you orders, Hooky?'

'The High Priestess of Hove. Your Tessa wasn't the only great character in the world, you know.'

'Are they ever going to find out who did it?'

'The police may not; possibly somebody else might.'

'It could have been somebody she gave a lift to. Tessa was a damned fool like that, she would give a lift to anyone if she thought they looked amusing, and "amusing" for her meant any really way out sort of character.'

'All characters can be way out at times,' Hooky said sombrely. 'We've all got a streak of madness in us.'

Mrs Dawson came back from the cellar with reinforcements; in due time the reinforcements were introduced into the firing line, Mrs Dawson herself being persuaded to join the celebrations.

'Well, here's all the best to you, Mr Hadleigh,' the good woman said, raising her glass. 'I'm sure you'll do well wherever you go.'

Hooky joined in the toast but privately took leave to doubt it. He was afraid the truth was that Lynton Hadleigh was one of those amiable chumps who would almost certainly make a mess of whatever situation he found himself in. There wouldn't always be someone on hand to put the stolen china back, Hooky thought.

Talk flowed, there was a deal of laughter and a little mild ribaldry; Martha Dawson, a glass of Moet et Chandon to

175

the good, said that she dearly liked to see two gentlemen enjoying themselves, it was like old times.

'What would go well after two bottles of champers, do you suppose?' Hadleigh wanted to know.

'A spot of fresh air and exercise,' Hooky told him.

'What horrible words! You can't seriously mean that, Hooky. What we'll do now is to climb into that lovely motor car of yours, drive to Otter Lodge and continue this excellent course of treatment.'

'We'll do nothing of the sort,' Hooky assured him. 'What do you suppose PC Chalky White is doing at this moment? He's in hiding, round the corner somewhere, waiting for us to come out. If we were fools enough to get into the Jag he'd be out in a flash with his breathalyser. Never stick your head into a noose if you don't have to, chum. What we'll do now is to walk up to Otter Lodge on our flat feet, in sober fashion, no singing and dancing en route, and when we get there I strongly recommend that you curl up in an armchair and sleep things off for an hour or so.'

By the time they reached Otter Lodge Hadleigh was beginning to feel that the armchair suggestion was a good one and his invitation to Hooky to come in and continue the festivities was only half-hearted. The soldier of fortune smilingly declined. 'Sufficient for the day is the bubbly thereof,' he pointed out. 'Off you go to your armchair and I'll take some more fresh air and exercise.'

That last visit which the detective paid to the shop seemed to change everything somehow. Well, not so much change everything as bring everything into focus, make things stand out more clearly. I began to get my own thoughts sorted out better. One odd thing is that I find myself going back a lot; I keep thinking of Aunt Mamie and of the time I lived with her and of what she used to tell me about the Elect People and about her dreams.

I dream a lot these days, but my dreams aren't as clear as they used to be; lately they've been mixed up a lot; I've seen

Eileen in them, and that's extraordinary, I never used to dream about her; and the detective sergeant has kept coming in, too, especially since that last visit of his. When that started happening I didn't like it at all until I remembered what Aunt Mamie always used to say, that dreams were sent as warnings, that the Lord used dreams to warn us. If the Lord was sending me a warning I had to take heed of it, and I kept turning over in my head the details of the detective's visit and worrying about it.

Why did he say *don't send Mrs Hudson away, it's all in the family*? I hadn't got a family. I never have had and never wanted one. I'm a loner. I didn't want to share anything with anybody. Especially not with Eileen. I didn't want her in my private world; the only world which meant anything to me, the world in which I was master of everything and in which nobody else and nothing else mattered. Or even existed; at times, the really good times, I felt like that – that nobody existed, that there wasn't anybody else except the Lord and me.

If they did exist, if they threatened me and got in the way they would have to be got out of the way. There was no escaping the logic of that. That's the beauty of serving the Lord, of getting messages from him, everything is logical, everything works up to an inevitable conclusion. You aren't troubled about whether you should do the thing or not, you have to do it.

And why had he asked about O'Donovan's? Why should that matter? What conclusion could they possible draw from the fact that I had decided not to go there any more? And who had put them on to it, if it wasn't Eileen? Eileen had found out I wasn't going to the gymnasium any longer; had she said anything about it to the police? Had she been having friendly little chats with Sergeant Wilson ('it's all in the family') that I knew nothing about? Just as I didn't really know what she and that cousin of hers chatted about every time she slipped down there for a cup of tea, except that I knew they talked about Barwold. For some reason or other Eileen must have been thinking a lot about Barwold. At any rate when the detective was in the shop and Dolly Winter's name was mentioned she suddenly asked '*wasn't she the girl who was buried at Barwold?*'

More and more I realised that I would have to tread warily, that people whom I didn't want in my private world were threatening that world, were getting between me and the Lord and that I would have to do something about it. But I would have to be careful. I knew that if I waited, bided my time, I would get a message of some sort, an opportunity would be given me and it would be up to me to take it.

The immediate thing was not to scare Eileen, which was why, when the detective left the shop after that last visit, I paid her a compliment about the way she made tea. I told her she made a nice cup of tea. Actually it's true, she does, but it's not the sort of thing I would take the trouble to tell her normally.

I was careful not to overdo it, I didn't want her to start getting suspicious, but every now and again I said something pleasant and instead of sitting without speaking, which was our normal way of going on, I tried to chat a bit.

I noticed that she wasn't 'slipping down' to see that cousin of hers and was pleased about it; the less those two women gossiped together the better as far as I was concerned. I asked Eileen why she hadn't been going down to see her cousin and she told me that Connie was on holiday at Bournemouth; I didn't know what Bournemouth had done to deserve her, but long may she stay there I thought.

A week or ten days went by and nothing much happened, the detective didn't come back, and since cousin Connie was away Eileen didn't have much opportunity for gossiping. I was still having my dreams and now Eileen came into them more than ever, but in a curious way and in a way I didn't like although it fascinated me. I knew it was Eileen, and yet when she turned to look at me it wasn't her face, it was the faces of the two whores the Lord told me to deal with mixed up together and grinning at me.

Having to be down at the station to collect the papers off the early train I am always about in the shop when the first post arrives. Usually it's a matter of bills or receipts or circulars, very seldom any private letters. But on this particular morning there was a letter addressed to Eileen. The postmark was 'Bournemouth' so I knew whom it was from and I was curious to know what that cousin of hers was writing about.

I slipped the letter into my pocket and didn't say anything to Eileen about it.

Later in the morning when she had gone round to the greengrocer to do some shopping I took the envelope out and opened it.

> Dear E
>
> Here we are at Bournemouth and the weather isn't too bad, wet yesterday but sunny today. The place doesn't seem to change much, though everything is more expensive, they certainly know how to charge here! But mustn't grumble, I suppose, as it's very comfortable and the food good.
>
> I've been thinking about you a good deal and wondering how you've been getting on with that husband of yours. Is everything OK? I get funny feelings at times as you know. I don't know how you stick him E, really I don't after some of the things you've told me about him. Though I must say we've had one or two good laughs together about him.
>
> What about that nice man from Barwold who keeps coming in to see you? Any developments there?
>
> We've a week more here so see you when I get back.
>
> Love, C.

I read through the letter again slowly and it was obvious

how right I had been to open it. *One or two good laughs* – well, I didn't mind that, I knew who was going to have the last laugh; *that nice man from Barwold who keeps coming in to see you* – that could only be the chap I knew as Hooky, the one Eileen had described as tall and well built (which was a sneer at me, of course); according to Connie he keeps coming in. What does he keep coming in about? About something at Barwold? And why hasn't Eileen told me about him?

I put the letter away in my pocket. I would have to dispose of it later, which would be a matter of a few seconds; thinking over its contents and making up my mind what to do about them would take longer.

Two days later Eileen said, 'I wonder how Connie is getting on at Bournemouth; I've been expecting to hear from her.'

'Maybe she has written and it's gone astray,' I told her, 'you know what posts are nowadays.'

It was in the evening of that same day, the day she wondered about not hearing from her cousin, that she spotted the advertisement in the *Courier*. She reads the *Evening Courier* from first page to last, all the news items and most of the advertisements as well.

'It's the Pageant at Arling Manor on Thursday,' she exclaimed.

Arling Manor is a big house some nine or ten miles from Dunsly. It is open to the public two days a week and once a year they have this Historical Pageant in the grounds. I had never been to it personally, but lots of people did go, and I suppose, if you like that sort of thing, it makes a good day out.

Eileen might have made that remark to me a dozen times and I wouldn't have paid any attention to it, would scarcely have heard it because she has this annoying habit, when she is looking at the evening paper, of reading bits out loud, which infuriates me because my thoughts are always busy about other things, about my own affairs and about what the Lord wants me to do; and I don't want to be bothered with Eileen's silly chatter about something which doesn't matter in the least. But this time I did pay attention. There was a sort of click in my brain. Uncertainty cleared away, like a mist rolling aside and instead of wondering what I was going to do and how I was going to do it *I knew*. This was it. I had never been to Arling Manor, but I knew where it was. I knew what road to take to it. And I knew exactly where I was going to turn off along the road.

'The Arling Pageant,' I said, 'would you like to go to it?'

'Would you really take me?' Eileen asked. She was astonished. I hadn't suggested taking her out anywhere for years. She was so surprised that for a moment I felt sorry for her. My mind was already completely made up on what I was going to do. There could be no going back on that. But just for a moment I could afford to feel sorry, as much, I suppose, for myself as for her. Love? I have never understood much about love. Certainly there had never been any between myself and Eileen. And precious little tenderness or affection. I hadn't wanted things like that, I thought I was better off without them. Probably I was. It was what the Lord had ordained. Things were better that way, but just for a moment, and knowing now what was going to happen to her, I could feel sorry for this silly woman who had missed so much.

'Why not?' I said. 'We don't often go out' (which was an understatement if ever there was one)!

'What about the shop?'

'We'll open in the morning as usual till twelve o'clock and then shut it for the afternoon. Why shouldn't we for once?'

She could hardly believe it. 'It would be marvellous,' she said. 'I should love to go. I've no idea what I shall wear.'
Wear a shroud, I might have told her, wear a shroud. . . .

As it happened, that Thursday morning was unusually busy and Eileen actually wondered whether we ought to shut with so many people coming in.

I soon put a stop to that. 'Don't be silly,' I told her. 'You want to see the Pageant, don't you?'

'Yes I do, dreadfully.'

'Then stop nattering. We'll shut up now and as soon as we've had a bite of something we'll be off.'

When we were getting in the car Eileen, now all excitement, said, 'I don't know the way to Arling, do you?'

I told her yes, I knew the way, not to worry.

I don't like people talking to me when I am driving, especially if my mind is busy about important things, but there was no stopping Eileen that afternoon: would there be many people there? would we be able to park? had I got enough money? were we going to be in time; was I sure we were on the right road and all the rest of it. I told her not to worry, I knew the way; but unfortunately when we came to the fork which I had been waiting for she spotted the signpost.

'The signpost said the other way for Arling,' she exclaimed, 'and this way to Barwold.'

Well, she knew now, or at least she partially knew, so the only thing to do was to jolly her along.

'That's right,' I told her, 'it's all on the way; only a bit of a diversion; I thought you might like to go through Barwold.'

She didn't know what to make of this. She was silent for a few seconds and then said, 'Not particularly. Why should I?'

'You're always talking about the place,' I answered. 'I thought you would like to have a look at it.'

I think she realised then that something was wrong, but of course she didn't know exactly what, nor exactly how wrong. She stopped talking and I trod on the accelerator. I wanted to hurry on to the end now.

I knew where the lane we were in would lead me. It would suddenly turn a sharp corner. Nearly a right-angled bend and then I would see the high banks on either side and the tall trees arching over and making a green tunnel

182

just as I had seen them once before. Once before, when the whore's car had been there and she herself had been standing beside it. 'You funny little man,' she had said, 'I knew you would come in useful some day.'

It was the last thing she did say; the Lord told me to teach her a lesson and I did.

That's what I had to do, teach women that they couldn't interfere with my way of life and with the work I had to do for the Lord.

I had to teach this one to stop being inquisitive about Barwold, I had to prevent her talking behind my back to the man called Hooky and possibly to the police. . . .

'What are we stopping for?' she asked, and now she was frightened. . . .

When Hooky parted from Lynton Hadleigh at Otter Lodge he was in great form. Renewing acquaintance with Messrs Moet et Chandon in the Ram had done him good. 'Fresh air and exercise' had been his prescription for Hadleigh, and Hooky now proposed to continue that excellent course of action himself.

Otter Lodge stood at one end of Barwold and having seen Hadleigh safely inside Hooky partially retraced his steps through the village. He did not propose to go as far as the Ram, which he thought might strain his good resolutions too far, but he was looking for a turning, left or right, some hitherto unexplored lane which would serve as a start for the cross-country walk he was determined to take.

Just such a turning and PC White came into view simultaneously. The constable was on foot pushing his bicycle; he looked hot and cross.

'Given up riding?' Hooky enquired amiably, 'or haven't you quite mastered the trick of it yet?'

'Puncture,' Chalky announced in disgust. 'Some fool has broken a bottle all over the road outside the Ram. I suppose that's where you are going back to?'

Hooky beamed at him, not one whit disconcerted by the

question. 'Ultimately, yes, no doubt,' he said, 'but immediately, no. Immediately I am about to embark on a long country walk.'

'Very nice too, I should say. Where are you going?'

'Like the rest of mankind I haven't the vaguest idea,' Hooky answered, and pointing he asked, 'where will that take me?'

'World's End.'

Hooky laughed immoderately. 'I wouldn't be at all surprised,' he said, 'the way everybody is carrying on. I must certainly go and see what happens at the end of the world. Mind you don't get attacked by any savage little white dogs on your way home, Chalky.'

PC White was not amused.

World's End turned out to be not a village, not even a hamlet, merely a dilapidated farm with a pair of even more dilapidated cottages neaby. A grubby little girl was busy skipping in front of one of the cottages. The advent of a stranger was clearly a matter of grave suspicion to her. She suspended her skipping and stared at the intruder.

The lane which had brought Hooky to World's End now petered out into no more than a footpath. Hooky pointed to this and asked, 'Where does that lead to?'

'Nowhere?' the seven-year-old replied and resumed her skipping.

In a sense nowhere was exactly where Hooky wanted to go. He had no set target in mind; he wanted to explore the countryside for maybe a couple of hours and to work off some of his superfluous energy.

He set off along the path to nowhere with the vague idea of keeping generally on a right-hand course and so eventually coming back somewhere in the neighbourhood of known parts.

World's End Farm was behind him now. Now there were no buildings, no humans, no traffic noise. He was alone, walking on the short, sweet grass in silence, with black-faced sheep eyeing him warily as he passed.

As he walked his thoughts ranged over all that had happened since he had come to Barwold and installed himself in the friendly Ram. Tessa came to his mind first – Tessa with so much potential for good in her but with a fatal streak, the worst possible partner Lynton Hadleigh could have chosen for himself, not that he did much of the choosing, Tessa would see to that, Hooky thought, but not unkindly; it was difficult to think unkindly of a twenty-two-year-old girl whose life had been savagely throttled out of her.

He thought of Tessa's father. The gent, one of the endangered species, with the thought of what had happened to his daughter and of what was happening to his wife locked in his heart, still trying to live life decently and normally, and he remembered a quotation from somewhere about most men living lives of quiet desperation.

That thought about quiet desperation led him to speculate about the shop in North Street; plenty of quiet desperation there, he was prepared to wager; was it just normal feminine jealousy that fretted the woman, or did she suspect something? and if she suspected something, or somebody, exactly what and whom and why? The memory came back to him of the figure in Barwold churchyard staring down at the grave of a murdered woman and for a second he felt again the cold *frisson* which had once seized him.

He thought of Chalky White the conscientious plodder and he smiled slightly, and of Chalky's superiors Messrs Marsh and Wilson, honest hardworking policemen even if they were private eye haters. He thought of the upright old woman in Hove whose friendship with Harry Fellingham had been the *fons et origo* of the whole affair and he wished the old lady, so crammed full of common sense, was at hand to be consulted about what best to do next.

He emerged from these pleasant mental ramblings to the realisation of two less pleasant facts; *a*, that the day had turned traitor and what had been a sunny sky when he started out was now giving every evidence of being about to pour with rain; and *b*, that he was well and truly lost. His theory had been that by keeping steadily on a right-hand course he would eventually cut across the road which led back to Barwold; but no such road had yet appeared, nor did any such road seem likely to appear. He had just made his way through a sizeable spinney of beech trees and was standing on the edge of a huge ploughed field without any idea of which way he should go.

'Lost yourself then, Mr Hefferman?'

The words made Hooky jump, so convinced had he been that he was utterly alone. He swung round and a friendly figure materialised from behind the hedge.

'Good Lord, George, what are you doing here? And where are we for Pete's sake? I've been expecting to meet a band of Eskimos at any moment.'

George Dawson laughed. 'No Eskimos round here, Mr Hefferman,' he said. 'At least not as I know about. Not on Westgate Farm.'

'Is that where I am, Westgate Farm?'

'That's it. Mr Nash's. Where I get the corn from for the poultry. He can't make head or tail of one of these Ministry forms and I promised I'd give him a hand trying to sort it out, which is enough to give anyone a headache, I may tell you. I would have driven over, of course, but the car's gone dodgy again so I walked across the fields, it isn't all that distance if you know the way.'

'Which I didn't,' Hooky said. 'I ought not to have started out without a compass and a thick slab of chocolate. Thank heavens you've turned up. It's going to pour with rain, isn't it?'

George cocked a countryman's eye at the sky. 'Might do,' was his verdict, 'but I don't think we shall get much till the wind shifts. Still, it might be wiser to go back by the road.'

'If we can find the road,' Hooky said. 'I had just about given up hope of ever seeing a road again.'

George Dawson laughed. 'Things are often nearer than

you think,' he said. 'We are only a couple of fields off the Barwold road at this moment.'

'Lead on,' Hooky said, 'the sooner we get back to the Ram and to one of your mother's excellent Cotswold teas the better.'

'Ma knows how to cook a bit,' George admitted complacently.

'Your mother has a genius for cooking,' Hooky reprimanded him sharply. 'Never marry a woman who can't cook, George.'

'I don't fare to marry at all,' George said. 'I can't be bothered with women; when you add it up there's a lot of trouble attached to them.'

Hooky was forced to laugh. What a lamentable heresy, he thought. Trouble? Of course women meant trouble – delicious, delightful, diverting and sometimes dangerous trouble.

'It'll be heavy going across the plough,' George predicted, 'we'd best stick to the headland.'

They followed the headland round the plough and eventually by way of a gate in the far corner came into a small pasture field.

'If old Basher's here we shall have to run for it,' George remarked easily.

'Who's old Basher?'

'Mr Nash's Hereford bull.'

To Hooky's relief old Basher was elsewhere and their passage diagonally across the meadow was peaceful. There was a stile in the boundary hedge and approaching it George gave a word of warning. 'Mind getting over the stile, Mr Hefferman, it's a steep bank down into the lane.'

The banks on either side of the sunken lane were indeed steep, and the trees crowning them arched overhead to make a green tunnel. At the corner where the lane took a sharp bend a car was standing.

George grinned. 'Bit of slap and tickle going on there I shouldn't wonder,' he said, but Hooky hardly heard him;

187

he had seen and recognised the number plate of the car.

Something was happening inside the little saloon car; there was confused movement in it and a half-choked scream rang out. Shouting something, he himself was not sure what, Hooky rushed forward. . . .

'So what you are saying, Hefferman, is that it was pure coincidence that you were in that particular spot at that particular time?'

'It was a fortuitous concatenation of circumstances, Inspector.'

'I didn't know they taught you such long words where you went to school. What circumstances? I would like to hear exactly what you did yesterday afternoon.'

'What, again?'

'If you don't mind; by constant repetition the truth sometimes emerges.'

'You haven't much opinion of poor old human nature, Inspector.'

'None whatever,' Inspector Marsh replied. 'Poor old human nature spends its time robbing banks, mugging old ladies, setting fire to heavily insured homes, blowing up embassies, sticking knives into people and blowing holes in them; and on the whole doing pretty well out of the proceeds. It's my business to try to limit these activities. That's why I would like to hear again about your movements yesterday. I understand, and I can't say that I'm surprised, they started in the Ram.'

'Where else?'

'With Mr Lynton Hadleigh?'

'Who was in great form. He had just found someone mug enough to buy his antiques business and was in the mood to celebrate.'

'And you celebrated with him?'

'Inspector, I hadn't the heart to see him do it all on his own.'

'And when these celebrations came to an end were you sober?'

Hooky smiled amiably at the inspector. 'Sober enough not to get into my car,' he answered. 'Your man Chalky was waiting round the corner with his little breathalyser.'

'So what happened?'

'I saw Hadleigh safely back to Otter Lodge and advised him to curl up in an armchair and sleep it off. Personally I didn't feel like sleeping anything off. I felt like fresh air and some exercise. After all, there's nothing like a new experience, is there? I thought a country walk, maybe three or four miles, would do me good.'

'Where were you going to walk to?'

'Anywhere; nowhere.' Hooky laughed and said, 'Actually that's what the kid I saw skipping told me the path led to, 'nowhere,' she said, so I went along it intending to keep bearing right handed with the idea that eventually I would come back onto the Barwold road; but as things turned out I got well and truly lost. I ought to have had a compass. Were you ever a Scout, Inspector? Do you know how to find the north without a compass?'

Inspector Marsh shook his head.

'Place a stick in the ground,' Hooky told him, 'watch it all day and when the shadow turns to the east it's the north.'

Marsh received this useful piece of information without evident enthusiasm and asked, 'What next?'

'Luckily George Dawson popped up out of a hedge and told me we were on Westgate Farm and he would show me the way home. We crossed a couple of fields, climbed over a stile, slid down the steep bank into the lane and there the car was.'

'You recognised it?'

'I knew the number.'

'And what was happening?'

'It was difficult to tell exactly, but it was obvious that some sort of rumpus was going on inside and when I heard a woman scream I thought I had better investigate.'

Ten minutes later, after answering several more questions, Hooky took his leave and Marsh sat looking across at his subordinate.

189

'Sounds OK to me,' Sergeant Wilson said. 'He could be telling the truth.'

'Accidents do happen,' Marsh allowed. 'Trust a private eye to get mixed up in things somehow.'

'The person we've got to worry about is Hudson.'

Marsh nodded. 'True enough,' he agreed, 'true enough. It's all a bit tricky at the moment.'

'He certainly assaulted his wife; we can hold him on that for a bit anyway but it's these self-accusations I don't like. He's already claimed to have done the Wardle Gardens murder and to have killed the Fellingham girl; according to him it's what the Lord told him to do and he's proud to have done it. But a man can't give evidence against himself, and he's just as likely to turn round tomorrow and deny the whole thing.'

'Do you think he did the two jobs?'

'His wife thought he was going to strangle her and the other two were strangled, so he might have done. On balance I'd say he probably did; but I'd give odds against ever getting him in jail. If he isn't actually mad counsel for the defence will certainly claim that he is; and prison's no good to him anyway, the best thing to do is to get him put in a home of some sort out of the way and let the call girls get on with their legitimate business uninterrupted.'

Inspector Marsh sighed. 'You're probably right,' he admitted, 'and the worst of it is it will mean a hell of a lot of paper work.'

In Regency House Roly Watkins said, 'Nice to see you back, guv; I was beginning to think we had lost you for ever.'

Hooky shook his head, smiling. 'I'm a Cockney bird, Roly, a London sparrow. The old slattern is home for me,. and I shall always come back to her – home is the sailor home from the sea and the hunter home from the hill.'

'Enjoyed your little stay in the wilds, did you?'

'It had its ups and downs.'

'That's what the girl told the soldier. Locals hostile, were they?'

'Not all of them.'

'Some funny goings on according to the papers.'

Hooky smiled; taken by and large he reckoned that 'some funny goings on' was a pretty good description of life and of the way human beings conducted their affairs.

'Yes, some funny goings on,' he agreed.

'And you let yourself get mixed up in them naturally; trust you, guv; never learn, do you? And it isn't as though you were eighteen any longer, is it?'

'Ever at my back I hear Time's winged chariot hurrying near.'

'Well, there you are, guv; if you've started hearing voices and things it's a sign, it's a warning. Wine, women and song, that's your trouble, isn't it? Always has been. Admitted you've gone off song a bit lately; which is a blessing all round; and now it's time to ease up on the wine and the women. Give the high-flyers a miss, guv, high-flyers get themselves into trouble.'

They do indeed, Hooky thought, they get themselves strangled by religious maniacs. 'Religion, what excesses are committed in thy name,' he exclaimed.

'You've slobbered a bibful there, guv,' Roly agreed fervently. 'If you're going to get religion I'm off.'

'Stop talking nonsense,' Hooky said, 'and go down and see what the postman has just brought.'

The second post of the day had just been delivered and after a visit to the ground floor Roly returned with a single letter.

'Despatches from foreign parts,' he announced. 'Look out.'

Whether Hove could rightly be described as foreign parts Hooky wasn't sure, but that was where the letter came from.

My dear nephew,

Yesterday I braced myself for the ordeal of a visit to London – now no longer a pleasure, there are too many people in the world. The three or four decent shops that one used to know are now no better than Church bazaars, with a strong Eastern flavour about them.

But I didn't go to do shopping, I went to see Harry Fellingham. And with Harry some remnants of civilised living still exist – a glass of Madeira wine and a dry biscuit at eleven o'clock amongst them. Poor Harry! – that dreadful business about his daughter and Nancy dying of cancer. But of course he keeps his standards, he faces up to things.

He told me that you have been to see him and have been kind and helpful over his troubles, especially about Tessa. I write this letter therefore, my dear Hooky, to say *well done*. I am well aware that you regard me as a tiresome, complaining old woman. Most of the time I no doubt am. But not always, not today. Today I am not complaining, I am complimenting you for being nice to Harry.

Your affectionate aunt,
Theresa Page-Foley

P.S.   I noticed your name mentioned in the paper in connection with the affair at Barwold; please do your best to avoid such unpleasant publicity, I do not care to see members of the family named in the cheap press.

T. P-F

'Bad news?' Roly enquired as Hooky put the letter away. 'No. On the whole, good news,' Hooky told him. 'News deserving a mild celebration.'

'Umbles or El Vino's?' Roly enquired.

'Probably a bit of both,' Hooky announced.

Roly shook his head.